The Anchor
and the
Journalist

OTHER BOOKS BY THE AUTHOR

LEAPING INTO THE SKY
FLEET
AXIS ALLY
A TARNISHED ROSE
AMERICAN STORIES
BLUE JACKETS
THE SAILOR AND TEACHER
HARLEM ON THE WESTERN FRONT
THE FORGOTTEN CHAPLAIN
IN THE WAKE OF THE EMPRESS OF CHINA
THE CONSPIRACY OF 1910 TO SAVE THE WORLD
TRAVELS WITH ERNIE
A DEAN'S LIFE

The Anchor
and the
Journalist

Robert Livingston

THE ANCHOR AND THE JOURNALIST

iUniverse books may be ordered through booksellers or by contacting:

iUniverse
1663 Liberty Drive
Bloomington, IN 47403
www.iuniverse.com
844-349-9409

ISBN: 978-1-6632-2265-7 (sc)
ISBN: 978-1-6632-2266-4 (e)

Print information available on the last page.

iUniverse rev. date: 05/26/2021

CONTENTS

PART III
Under Attack

PART IV
Tall Tales

PART V
Bogies

PART VI
Twilight

DEDICATION

*TO THE GALLANT MEN AND SHIPS OF
RADAR PICKET STATION 10*

A FEW WORDS

On May 3, 1945 during the battle for Okinawa an American warship, the U.S.S. *Aaron Ward (DM-34)* was attacked by a flight of Japanese kamikaze planes. The attack began at 6:22 p.m.(1822) and lasted 52-minutes. Inexplicably, seven suicide planes, though heavily damaged by furious anti-aircraft fire, still crashed onto the *Aaron Ward* and all but sank the ship. Forty-two crewmembers were killed and many more were wounded. One of those killed was Laverne Schroeder, just two months before his eighteenth birthday. To remember their son, the Schroeder family of Elgin, Illinois purchased an anchor from the Navy once the destroyer was sold for junk in 1946. In time the anchor was placed in the military section of the Bluff City Cemetery in Illinois. There the anchor remained, a silent reminder of what took place in an invisible nautical box denoted as RPS-10 during the last great battle of World War II. This is the story of the *Aaron Ward's* gallant fight, a brave young man, and a reporter's quest to honor the ship's legacy.

LAVERNE SCHROEDER

NAVAL TIME – WATCHES

The Navy uses a 24-hour clock. This story takes place during at the Second Dog Watch, 1822, or 6:22 p.m.

MID-WATCH	FORENOON WATCH	FIRST DOG WATCH
0000 – MIDNIGHT	0800 – 8:00 AM	1600 – 4:00 PM
0100 – 1:00 AM	0900 – 9:00 AM	1700 – 5:00 PM
0200 – 2:00 AM	1000 – 10:00 AM	1800 – 6:00 PM
0300 - 3:00 AM	1100 – 11:00 AM	
0400 – 4:00 AM	1200 – 12 NOON	

MORNING WATCH	AFTERNOON WATCH	SECOND DOG WATCH
0500 – 5:00 AM	1300 – 1:00 PM	**1800 – 6:00 PM**
0600 – 6:00 AM	1400 – 2:00 PM	1900 – 7:00 PM
0700 – 7:00 AM	1500 – 3:00 PM	2000 – 8:00 PM
0800 – 8:00 AM	1600 – 4:00 PM	

NIGHT WATCH

2000 – 8:00 PM

2100 – 9:00 PM

0000 – MIDNIGHT

2200 – 10:00 PM

2300 -- 11:00 PM

2400 -- 1200 MIDNIGHT

NAVAL TIME

1300 – 1:00 PM

0100 – 1:00 AM	1400 – 2:00 PM
0200 - 2:00 AM	1500 – 3:00 PM
0300 – 3:00 AM	1600 – 4:00 PM
0400 – 4:00 AM	1700 – 5:00 PM
0500 – 5:00 AM	**1800 - 6:00 PM**
0600 – 6:00 AM	1900 – 7:00 PM
0700 - 7:00 AM	2000 – 8:00 PM
0800 – 8:00 AM	2100 9:00 PM
0900 – 9:00 AM	2200 – 10:00 PM
1000 – 10:00 AM	2300 – 11;00 PM
1100 – 11;00 AM	2400 – 12 MIDNIGHT
1200 – 12 NOON	0000 - MIDNIGHT

Part I

HONORING THE SACRIFICE

BATTLE OF OKINAWA 1945 – APRIL 1 TO JUNE 22

368 SHIPS DAMAGED

36 SHIPS SUNK

4,907 OFFICERS AND SAILORS KILLED

4,582 U.S.ARMY KILLED

2,792 U.S. MARINES KILLED

45,000 TOTAL WOUNDED

100,000 JAPANESE KILLED

Chapter 1

APRIL FOOLS DAY

San Francisco, 1995 - March

Every year has been the same for nearly five decades. The calendar's pages, blown by the winds of time, revealed an old shipmate buried deep within me, who returned to spin a wild sea yarn, and to again remind me and others of a day long ago.

April 1st swings by and those darn goose bumps still erupt on the back of my neck and cause, especially in the last few years, my few remaining hairs to stand on end in a choreographed dance of frightful memories. Over the years my family got used to it, my wife Jean and our grown kids, Thomas and Ruth.

And really, what could they do about it? Short of being stricken with amnesia on my part, or the first day of April being discarded by the world's calendar makers, I was in for it each year. My wife understood my annual descent into the past. She still had the letters I wrote her so long ago from Okinawa and, of course, she had seen the newsreels at the movie theaters. What we call television was on the horizon and not yet in our living rooms. Given the slaughterhouse that was the battle for the island that was probably a good thing. Yes, she knew all too well why her husband got a little jumpy as that darn month approached. And, as you might expect, after awhile the kids came to understand why their dad acted as he did.

Over the years the family had sat through many evenings when old shipmates came by to chat about one particular day, May 3,1945 when the Pacific war compressed itself into a 52-minutes of living hell in the waters off of Okinawa. Naturally, the kids couldn't believe the stories they heard; they were just too unbelievable. As they got older I showed them the official Navy photographs of the ship, grainy black and white pictures and their doubts evaporated. They knew beyond doubt that their father had been on the ship prowling the South China Sea, and they knew what happened. Seven Japanese kamikaze planes, seeking suicide for glory, attacked the *USS Aaron War (DM-34)* as she patrolled the invisible box called Radar Picket Station – 10 (RPS-10).

Two photographs always claimed their attention. The first photo showed the newly minted and untested ship leaving San Pedro, California for sea trails before heading to Pearl Harbor and points westward. The second photo showed what happened on May 3rd. It's difficult to believe, the kids always thought, that the photos were of the same ship.

The kids also knew the background to the *Ward*. Her keel was laid down on December 12, 1943 by the Bethlehem Shipbuilding Company. She was launched on May 5, 1944 and commissioned later on October 1944. The *Ward* was designated a destroyer minelayer (DM-34). The ship was 376 feet in length and displaced 2,200 tons. She was capable of 34 knots or about 39 mph. Her complement included 363 officers and enlisted men. Commander William H. Sanders was the commander of the *Ward*. The kids also knew that 42 crewmembers were lost on May 3, 1944. Those deaths and the *Ward's* stubborn resistance to the Japanese kamikaze attacks led to a fateful commendation from Fleet Admiral Chester Nimitz, who said, "We all admire a ship that can't be licked."

THE WARD AFTER THE ATTACK

The kids also knew that their father, Robert Rosenthal, though seriously wounded, had survived the greatest threat to the US Navy in World War II, the Japanese suicide campaign. Japan would trade a plane for an American ship in the death throes of the Imperial Empire.

KAMIKAZE ATTACK

The kids knew two other things about the ship. The Navy sold the ship to scrap iron dealers in 1946. At the request of a family in Illinois, one of the ship's anchors was sold to them for $25.00.

"Robert, you're going, aren't you?
"I spoke to Lansing last month."
"And?"
"He wants to go to Elgin."
"On May 3rd?"
"Yes."

Robert Rosenthal was speaking quietly to his wife, Jean in the warmth of their kitchen. As they did, they sipped tea and occasionally enjoyed small bite of an their apple turnovers.

"You've told the kids?"
"You mean our thirty-plus offspring with kids of their own?"
"Yes, Robert, unless you haven't told me about others."
"Yes."
"They want you to go?"
"Yes. You?"
"I think you must."
"We're the last two."
"I know. And it's the fiftieth anniversary and at 72 you're not getting any younger."
"Jean, the kids remembered Lansing."
""Of course they did. Who would forget Uncle Murray?"

Murray Lansing wasn't really an uncle by blood, but he was by his frequent visits over the years. He always brought presents for the children, a smart handshake for the man-of-the-house, and a robust hug for Jean.

"I think Murray had a crush on you, honey."
"He was, I recall, a rather handsome man."

4

"But slow. I beat him to your doorstep."
"Barely, Robert."

"I couldn't afford all those hats he always brought you."
"I still have a bewildering collection."
"Donate them to Goodwill."
"What? They're keepsakes."
"How did I ever win you over?"
"Your charm as a reporter."

I wasn't sure about the charm bit. As to being a reporter, all too true. It began in high school, Balboa High in San Francisco. I took a journalism class at the urging of my school counselor. Mr. Peterson was a great teacher and I took to the class like the proverbial fish to water. In time I became the paper's editor before graduation. Then it was off to four years at the University of San Francisco (USF), a wonderful Jesuit school. There Father Harry Flannigan pushed a nice Jewish kid to write, join the school paper, and graduate with a major in journalism. All this I did before the draft board finally caught up with me and, at my request, dropped me off in the US Navy. That was sometime in mid-1943, around April. A year later I was on the *U.S.S. Ward,* placed there by the War Department to help record the ship's history during Operation Iceberg.

What kind of name is Operation Iceberg for, as it turned out, the last great battle of World War II? Are we talking about lettuce for a dinner salad or 1500 Allied ships with over half a million sailors, Marines, and Army personnel attacking an island fortress just 340 miles from Japan proper? I never understood why the name was chosen, not with 12,000 American dead at sea and on land, and over 50,000 casualties. And then, of course, there were the Japanese dead, 100,000 soldiers and a half-million civilians. The plan should have been called Operation Slaughterhouse. That's what it was, 82-days of killing for a piece of real estate the smaller than Los Angeles County. It was also the last steppingstone on the way to Tokyo. Any invasion of Japan would begin on Okinawa and promised to be bloody.

THE SEVERELY DAMAGED U.S.S. AARON WAR - 1945

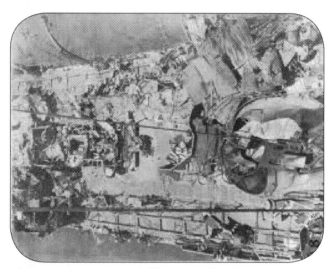

THE U.S.S. AARON WARD'S DAMAGED DECK

The map declared and defined the Naval Battle of Okinawa and justified the struggle of the gallant radar picket ships that fought off the greatest suicide attack of the Pacific War. One of those ships was the *U.S.S. Aaron Ward* and I was on her deck on May 3, 1945.

Chapter 2

ELGIN

Jean helped me pack for my trip to Elgin. First, she went down her survival list for me: credit cards, Medicare and Social Security cards, Auto Club card, AARP card, DMV card, and Mercury Auto Insurance card. Another card and I could have opened up my own casino.

Then came the personal items --- *Fruit of the Loom* necessities, toiletries, medications, vitamins, two pair of glasses, and three changes of clothing. You would have thought I was globe-hopping jetsetter. How Jean did it, I never understood. She worked miracles. Everything went into one reasonable manageable suitcase.

And at LAX, she went down her list of reminders: tickets, cash, and a list of phone numbers and addresses.

"I think you're ready," she said.
"You think so?"
"We'll see, won't we?"
"I'll call every night."
"You better. And one more thing."
"Yes?"
"No redheads."

"Me?"

"You."

We both laughed.

"O.K. What about a blond?"

"Only if she'll remind you to take your medications."

"That's a tough one."

"I thought so."

The P.A. system reminded me to find my boarding pass. After searching for it in all available pockets, Jean handed it to me. I was, it appeared, a little nervous.

"One more thing world traveler."

"Yes, Jean."

"Don't forget Murray's banana bread. It's in your carry-on."

"How could I?"

"Give him a big hug and kiss for me."

"I guarantee the hug."

"Party pooper."

We kissed and I boarded United, flight 122, for Chicago O'Hare Airport and my trek into the past.

The flight was uneventful, sort of. Three Scotch on the rocks made it so, as did the lovely flight attendant who took compassion on an obviously nervous passenger. Poor lady, she thought it was the rough weather over the Rockies, which was the cause of my drinking. It wasn't. I was reviewing days and dates related to the *Ward*, periodic notations on past calendars and the ship's log that were insistent to be seen again.

The Ward's Cruise to Okinawa

February 9, 1945   Departed San Pedro for Pearl Harbor.

February 15, 1945   Arrived Pearl Harbor.

March 16, 1945	Ship underway to join the 5th Fleet in the Caroline Islands, some 360 miles from Guam.
March 19, 1945	Cruising with Task Force 52 bound for the Ryukyu Islands.
March 22, 1945	Ship arrived off Okinawa.
April 1, 1945	Ship supporting larger warships off Okinawa.
April 4, 1945	Departed Ryukyu Islands for the Marianas.
April 10, 1945	Arrived at Saipan.
April 27, 1945	Shot down one enemy plane off Okinawa.
April 30, 1945	Ship took up station at RPS10.
May 3,1945	Crew went to general quarters; bogies reported.

I spent two days in the *"windy city"* visiting old friends at the *Chicago Tribune* and catching a Cub game at Wrigley Field before picking up my rental at *Enterprise*, an off-brown, two-door Nissan coupe. The irony of driving a Japanese vehicle to Elgin, Illinois to recall a battle fought against the Emperor did not, of course, escape me.

Elgin was an old town, owing its origins to Congregationalists in the 1820's, who settled near the Fox River, approximately 40 miles west of Chicago's present day "miracle mile." Over the years, it played host to a number of businesses, including two icons: the *Elgin Watch Corporation*, and the *Borden Milk Company*. That's right, fine timepieces and condensed milk, pocket watches for retirees, and *Elmer's* glue for the kids. Half the watches produced in the country for almost a century, and *Elsie the Cow* on your doorstep each week. Today, both companies are gone like so many things.

Map in hand I drove to Elgin, and, after getting lost twice due, I might add, due to an obviously inaccurate map from *Rand McNally*, I found State Street and passed a sign welcoming visitors to the fastest growing residential town in northern Illinois. It's always nice to be welcomed in the late afternoon even if you are from NY or LA.

There was a light mist, which my wipers handled without difficulty Ahead of me, I finally saw it, the Elgin Naval Club, a square-looking 1950's building, where another vehicle was already parked, a flaming red-colored Ford Mustang.

Murray Lansing stood by it holding a black umbrella and wearing a big Irish smile as I slowed and stopped. Before exiting the Chevy, I dove into my carry-on for "you know what."

For a moment, we stood in the drizzle, two old shipmates; then we hugged.

"Here," I said, "Jean's finest."
"She didn't forget. What a woman!"
"I think so."
"Murray, I supposed to give you a big, sloppy kiss."
"Tell her I'll take a rain check."
"You got it."
"If you hadn't asked her, I would have."
"I was quicker, Murray."
"I let you win."
"Hell, you did."

We both laughed in the rain standing together under his large black umbrella. Then he needled. He couldn't resist.

"I see you're as flamboyant as ever. Nice rental. A bit on the wild side, isn't it?"
"I like to blend in."
"With that color, you'll disappear."
"Fifty years ago that would have been a miracle."
"On that one, I can't disagree. Still, let's drive my Mustang while we're in town."
"We wouldn't want to draw attention to ourselves."
"Right, Rob."

That was my nickname Murray had given me. Unless I was with him, I disowned it. Rob, what kind of name was that? Al Capone might like it or institutional brokers on Wall Street, but for me, no way. Heck, I even submitted unvarnished IRS returns.

Murray was three years older, a big guy, about 200 plus pounds of former football muscle. He had been raised in New York City before receiving a gridiron scholarship to Oregon State University, where he eventually graduated with an engineering degree. That background would serve him well as a radar officer when war came.

He was still a good-looking guy. He still had a full head of hair and it still crowned his rugged features and extraordinary smile. How I ever won Jean in our head-to-head tussle I'll never know.

After the war, he returned to the *"big apple,"* where he worked for Westinghouse, married twice, sired five kids, and generally had a full life. Currently, he was without a wife, which I kept in mind given his proclivity for banana bread.

Still needling, Murray said, "I see you're still buying your clothes from a catalog."
"Saves time and gas."
"I bet, Rob"
"I also do off the rack on coupon days. It's inexpensive and functional."
"Cheap, you mean."
"Discounted, Murray."
"Yeah."
"You?"
"Brooks Brothers."
"Classy."

The fun was over. We both knew that. We had come to do a job. It was time. We couldn't be late.

"It's almost 1700 hours --- 5:00 p.m. Time for the Second Dog Watch," I said while scanning my very old Elgin pocket watch.
"I see you remembered ship board time. Not bad for a journalist who forget to stay ashore."

"And a navy historian… Let's not forget that, old buddy."

"True."

"Fifty years ago today, Murray."

"Almost to the hour. Just before sunset."

"It's like a dream now, Rob."

"It was a nightmare."

The two men, greetings over, walked toward the front door to the Naval Memorial Building. They stopped at the door.

"We're the last two, Murray. All that's left of the crew."

"I wonder what happened to the others --- to the "Little Boys." I wonder how many of those guys from the *LSMR 195* are still kicking."

"A few, perhaps like us."

"Rob, do you think they're meeting today?"

"Hopefully."

"Let's go in. It's our last watch."

LSMR195

Chapter 3

THE PURCHASE

I led the way into the Naval Memorial Building. Murray carried a large cardboard box, which he placed on a chair. In fading dark ink there was a simple notation on the carton, *U.S.S. Aaron Ward --- Remembrance,* May 3, 1945.

The inside of the building was perfectly suited for the various clubs, which met there --- the American Legion, the Veterans of Foreign Wars, the Elks, the Masons, Kiwanis, and the Moose. There was a large hall with about ten round tables, a bar, and a dance floor. In the back was a large kitchen to prepare meals for the many special occasions hosted in the building.

"Murray, you've been dragging that box around for a long time."
"Every yearly reunion for over forty years."
"You've taken good care of it."
"Well, you clowns elected me Historian, forever it seems. What could I do?"
"Good point."
"Rob, who gets it when we're gone?"
"Our kids? A museum? The History Channel?"
"One of us will have to decide."
"But not today, Murray."

We sat down and a cheerful lady of ample proportions and a generous smile brought us black coffee.

"Anything stronger, fellows?"

"What do you have in mind, my dear?" Murray asked, smiling.

"The stew isn't bad."

"Probably not today," I said. "We've got to get over to the Bluff City Cemetery in a few minutes."

"Vets?"

"How can you tell?" Murray asked.

"Are you kidding?" was her quick response. "I'll be around if you need me."

"Before you go…"

"Yes."

"Do you recall an anchor that was once out front?"

"Of course."

"Did people ever wonder about it?"

"Not the old folks. They knew all about it. Not so much with the younger ones. They just wandered by it."

"Shame."

"You guys were on that ship, the *Ward*. I could tell the moment you walked in. You've got the look."

While he was talking, Murray was fumbling with old scrapbooks and loose photographs before locating the picture he wanted.

"Here it is, Rob, one of the reasons why we're here."

The photo showed an anchor and few links of chain resting beside a plaque in front of the Elgin Navy Memorial Building. The anchor and chain seemed strangely out of place, a ship's relics 1,000 miles from the sea, an artifact of another time, and an earlier war. He showed the photo to the waitress.

"That's it."

"Funny, isn't it, Murray, about this anchor and chain, that it should be here rather than the Brooklyn Naval Yard or Treasure Island?"

"Or Pearl Harbor. But the old man, Harry Schroeder, lived here and here the anchor and chain remained just across the river at the cemetery."

"The V.F.W. moved that iron there in '71 after keeping it outside this building for all those years."

"What was it the old man paid, Rob, $20.00 for the anchor and chain in 1946?"

"That was the going price for 4,000 pounds of scrap iron from the *Aaron Ward* then for the starboard anchor. Can you believe it?"

"Rob, just so the family could remember their son, Laverne."

"Lots of memories over there in the Bluff City Cemetery," the waitress added, her voice suddenly saddened."

"You have…"

"An older brother. Died near the Manchurian border during the Korean War. He never made it home.

The two men had no response. Wars come and go, but the pain is always the same.

THE ANCHOR OF THE U.S.S. WARD, BLUFF CITY CEMETERY

"The old man heard the government was going to scrap the *Ward*. He wanted something from the Navy to remember his son. The Navy was willing to part with a clock. That offer was rejected, Murray. The dad wanted something more and the Navy finally obliged."

"The anchor was shipped from the East Coast on a railroad flatcar. It arrived in Elgin on July 17, 1946. Initially, it was placed against an elm tree of the Schroeder farm outside of Elgin. In 1947 the anchor was donated to the Navy Club of Elgin. That was on Memorial Day in 1947. The anchor rested in front of the Navy Club until it closed."

"Murray, that caused us a little problem when we were doing our research. Remember, we couldn't find where the anchor was relocated."

"But you figured it out. It was moved to the Bluff City Cemetery. The anchor was placed on top of a hill in a section dedicated to veterans. Each year the City holds services on Memorial Day to remember those from Elgin who gave their lives for our country."

As if on cue the two old men clinked their coffee mugs, ever so lightly as they recalled all those who died on the *Aaron Ward* that fateful day so long ago.

"Rob, do you recall what the plaque said, the one adjacent to the anchor?"

"Got it right here, Murray."

Read from an unfolded piece of paper, Rob said:

> *THE SHIP'S ANCHOR FROM THE*
> *U.S.S. AARON WARD*
> *WAS PRESENTED TO*
> *NAVY CLUB OF ELGIN SHIP NO. 7*
> *BY*
> *MR. AND MRS. HARRY J. SCHROEDER*
> *IN MEMORY OF THEIR SON*
> *LAVERNE H. SCHROEDER*
> *SEAMAN SECOND CLASS*
> *U.S.N.R.*
> *KILLED IN ACTION – MAY 1945*
> *OFF OKINAWA*
> *WHILE SERVING ABOARD THE*
> *DESTROYER*

"Rob, it hardly seemed fair, government surplus for a son."

"We were all surplus that day."

"But we came home. Laverne didn't."

"I know, Murray."

"Let's get up to the cemetery."

"Grab the box."

The two old vets left, their black coffee, barely touched, but not so their emotions. Always a good tipper, Murray left an extra generous one for the waitress, who might in future days remember two old salts. They headed out of town, crossing first the Fox River, and then along a meandering county road to the Bluff City Cemetery.

As they drove out of town, Rob thought about his history of the *Aaron Ward*, published 35-years ago entitled *52-Minutes at RPS 10*. At the time he thought it was both a catchy title, as well as an appropriate one. Unfortunately, except for history buffs and research libraries, sales languished. Truth be told, he bought about 300 hundred copies himself and salted them away until Christmas. Fortunately, Jean's family was large and they had lots of friends between them. Guess what many receive from Santa?

The reviews were mixed with the exception of one group, surviving members of the *Aaron Ward's* crew. It was a best seller with them. I guess they liked the way he told their stories.

MURRAY'S STORY

He was the Radar Room Chief. Above his head, the radar antenna whirled very silently, day and night. It sent out invisible electronic beams, which reached miles out across the ocean, probing, always probing for any object big enough to bounce an echo back to the ship. In the CIC --- the combat information center --- his radar men peered into their glowing oscilloscopes, watching the thin green lines sweeping outward, always searching for what they didn't want to find, a sudden bright point of light, a blip that meant something was out there. The blip was watched. Which way was it moving? Were there others? Was this a raid? Was the Aaron Ward the target?" These were the questions Murray had to answer. He couldn't screw up. One mistake could get you killed. It was his job to protect the ship. Murray didn't make mistakes.

OUR HOME AT SEA- THE U.S.S. AARON WARD

Chapter 4

THE CEMETERY

Rob steadied myself as Murray's "hot rod" moved onto the inner cemetery road of the Bluff City Cemetery. The light drizzle, which followed them across the lazy Fox River, was slowly dissipating. A fluttering breeze came up, quietly and soothingly, like a soft woolen blanket on a cold night. A flaming ball, no longer hidden by the misty clouds, was descending on the western horizon. It was going to be a beautiful evening.

The cemetery was owned by the City of Elgin since 1889. A brochure about it claimed 108 acres of well-maintained grounds providing a peaceful setting for loved ones. Rob wondered, of course, if young Schroeder, not yet eighteen when he was killed, cared about the *"peaceful setting."*

"Look at all those flags, Murray."

Murray was driving along a tree-lined road through a portion of the cemetery dedicated to veterans. Small American flags had been placed along the roadside about every fifty yards. Grave markers and flower bouquets drifted by us. Ahead, at the highest point of the cemetery, was a rounded grass covered knoll atop which was a fifty-foot flagpole, and flying from it, *Old Glory*.

Murray found a parking place but left the engine running to listen to the radio for a moment. Joan Baez was singing one of his favorite 60's songs.

> *Where have all the flowers gone?*
> *Long time passing*
> *Where have all the flowers gone?*
> *Long time ago…*

"Nice lyrics. Rob."
"Yeah."
"Let's walk."

They surveyed the area around them. Nearby were two Civil War cannons and a stack of neatly placed iron balls. A tapered pillar stood next to the weapons honoring the men who fought at Gettysburg or Vicksburg. Tugging at Murray, they moved past this older war to find a newer conflict. Then we saw it; the anchor and chain rested on a cement slab molded into the grassy hill.

The anchor seemed like a creature from some lost world --- beached, motionless, inanimate.

"Old man Schroeder did a good thing."
"So did the V.F.W. What a view, Rob."
"You're right."

From our perch they could see across the countryside, the peaceful farms dotting the landscape and the town of Elgin itself bathed in the late afternoon's sun. Everything seemed so safe here. No angry Pacific waters could touch this valley. Or could they?

"It's 1822, Murray – 5:22 p.m. on the dot."

"As you say, Rob, on the dot."

> *Where have all the flowers gone?*
> *The girls have picked them everyone*
> *Oh, when will you ever learn?*
> *Oh, when will you ever learn?*

The two men walked over to the anchor. Murray put down the cardboard box he had carried from the car. Speaking in a practiced, formal tone, we said:

"We are the last living survivors of the U.S.S. Aaron Ward. We have come to this place to remember and honor what took place fifty years ago this hour --- to recall a battle forgotten to all except for those who were there. Now we remember our ship and the crew with a final salute."

A large sedan pulled up nearby. Two youngsters, a boy and girl, perhaps six and eight years of age, leaped from the car, followed by their parents, who took decisively more measured steps. The mother held a bouquet of colored spring flowers. A Bible was in the father's hands.

The family saw us. I speculated later what they must have thought?

"Mommy, what are those two old men doing?" asked the little girl.
"Don't stare, dear."
"Too old for Vietnam. Maybe Korea," the father said.
"Can we stand by the anchor, too?" the little boy asked.
"No son, we have to find my brother's gravesite," the mother said sadly.
"The Vietnam section is over there," the father whispered. "Let's go."

Watching them, I knew they would return many times.

"Rob, I don't mean to interrupt your thoughts…"
"Right. Where were we?"

"We come to remember one shipmate in particular Laverne Schroeder, who died two months before his eighteenth birthday aboard the U.S.S. Aaron Ward. We come to remember the youth who saved our ship."

Murray withdrew from his pocket a *Purple Heart* and numerous battle ribbons, which he placed next to the anchor.

As he did so, Rob removed from the carton an American flag and a sword. The flag was folded into the traditional triangular shape. The sword was bent and tarnished black, as if burned and blackened by some great blast. He placed both items next to the medal and ribbons.

The flag was old and burned along its edges, even torn in places. The white stars, if counted, would have numbered 46. The sword was vintage Spanish-American War, a veteran of President William McKinley's day and Admiral George Dewey's Asiatic fleet.

"Rob, do you have it?"

I pulled out a worn envelope and carefully removed a sheet of paper.
I read:

"The President of the United States takes pleasure in presenting the Presidential Unit Citation to the U.S.S. Aaron Ward for extraordinary heroism against the enemy on May 3, 1945 during the battle for Okinawa."

THE FAMILY REMEMBERS A BROTHER
(Laverne is on the left)

"Are you ready, Murray. It's time to go."
"We need to go to the Rock Island."
"To the veteran cemetery."
"Where Laverne rests."

Part II

THE CREW OF THE AARON WARD

There are no extraordinary men... just extraordinary circumstances that ordinary men are forced to deal with.

William Halsey

When asked what I am most proud of, I stick out my chest, hold my head high and state proudly, "I served in the United State Navy!"

John F. Kennedy

Chapter 5

RENDEZVOUS

I got to the *Ward* the hard way. First, I traveled in a noisy, uncomfortable DC-3 cargo plane to Pearl Harbor from San Francisco, then by a slow troop ship crammed with Marines to Tarawa, where I hitched a ride on a tanker full of bunker oil before being transferred to a *"small boy"* in the churning waters of the South China Sea. If "frequent flier points" had been available in those days, I would have been in great shape.

"Small boy; now is that anyway to describe a warship?" Actually, the nickname was very appropriate. Considerably larger than a rubber raft, but smaller than a destroyer, these ships, lacking any real armament or big guns, were the Navy's workhorse in the Pacific. War-related goods were carried by these lumbering ships thousands of miles into the very heart of the Imperial Japanese Empire. What trucks in the "red ball express" were to the infantry in North Africa and Europe, the LSMR was to the Navy.

AN LSMR – "A SMALL BOY"

I was on an amphibious craft, the *LSMR 195*, which qualified as a "small boy," as she tossed her way through a heavy, choppy sea, a metallic bucking bronco in a rodeo like no other. The *195* and I had an early morning rendezvous with the *Aaron Ward* at *RPS* 10, a radar picket station 70 miles west, northwest of Okinawa. The *195* was shaped like a cigar box, a necessary virtue since it carried every form of invasion supply --- jeeps, boxes of ammo, food, water, mortars, machine guns, artillery shells, and young men. Her large size and shape of the *195* permitted this. Compared to a destroyer, she was a sluggish swimmer. She was a plodder, not a thoroughbred racing along, as she did, at only 8 knots. As such, she was a sea-going truck..

On this day, except for her crew and a compliment of deadly rockets, she was no longer loaded to the gills. She was empty with only a little fuel and riding high in the water. The *"R"* in *LSMR* referred to the rockets and much more --- *"Landing Ships/ Materials/Rockets."* In her cargo hold she held 500 cases of unused rockets, which were scheduled for unloading the next day.

On the bridge were three men --- Captain Atwood, First Officer Verso, and a career sailor, Lopez. Anxiously, they were scanning the horizon. Somewhere ahead through the unclear mist was the *Ward*.

"Mr. Verso, where's our guest? We're almost at RPS 10. Twenty minutes at the most, I think."

"Below deck. Retching!"

"Well, we warned him. The *195* was no place for a journalist, especially for a USF undergrad."

"Does he know you attended CAL," Verso asked, smiling.

"No. I didn't want to add to his unhappiness."

"Journalist, my foot," Lopez said. "A PR guy, that's what he is, making the war look good for the folks back home."

"Thanks for the insight, Lopez," Verso countered.

Captain Atwood always reminded people of an accountant. He was a slim, quiet man, unassuming in his position, a technician constantly dealing with facts and figures, always analyzing and interpreting, figuring out that puzzle called war. As it was, he had been an accountant at the *Bank of America* before Pearl Harbor. Once in the service, he was sent to the Great Lakes Naval station for advance training, then to the Bureau of Naval Construction for a very short stint. I guess someone had to account for the cost-plus contracts. After that, the *195* took up his time.

Verso was the second in command, and completely opposite of the Captain in many ways. He was large, loud, and assuming, and a constant commentator on the absurdities of life. Before December 7th, he had built expensive customized boats for the wealthy. At one time, he thought, he would join that group if enough boats could be built. Now he was working for Uncle Sam. As it turned out, he banked with *"B of A."* It was a small world.

Lopez, born and raised in East Los Angeles, was everyman's sailor, a refugee of Mexico in El Norte. Life in the Navy had given him an irreverent view of the brass and bureaucratic regulations, but not Captain Atwood. Lopez enjoyed tamales and tacos, but the Navy, perhaps in retaliation, chose not to serve these dishes or his beloved fried beans. As to his banking, he was a Wells-Fargo guy.

All three were married and fathers, and constant letter writers. In the matter of progeny, Lopez was the clear leader. His wife read his letters to five kids.

"Why the V.I.P. treatment for this guy?" Lopez asked. "Does he have an in with Halsey? The President?"

The two officers looked at Lopez. They were used to his interruptions. Indeed, they looked forward to his critiques of the Navy, the common seaman's wisdom breaking up the tedium and tension of a watery battlefield. Before they could respond, their PR guest reentered their world.

I was pale, soaked, and bedraggled. That can happen when the world moves beneath your feet and a heavy mist coats you on the way to the bridge. Lopez handed me a towel and a steaming mug of hot coffee.

"Ask him, Captain," Lopez suggested with a smile.
"Ask me what?"
"Why the V.I.P. treatment?" Verso asked.

I stared blankly at Verso. I wasn't even sure why I was here. One day I editing the *Stars and Stripes* in San Francisco, the next day I headed for Honolulu. Go figure. Still, I had to say something.

"President Roosevelt wants to keep the home fires glowing. People are tired of the war. Nazi Germany is almost gone, but the Japanese remain. The country is nervous. Christ, over 5,000 men lost to take Iwo Jima and now Okinawa and these damn suicide planes."

"Kamikazes," said Verso.
"The Divine Wind?"
"Mr. Rosenthal, there's nothing divine about them," added Lopez. "The bastards are trying to sink our ships. Dying for the Emperor by crashing into us."
"As to the P.R. treatment, Mr. Rosenthal?" the Captain asked.
"Beats me. The truth is, I think, they were looking for a young, unmarried, somewhat neurotic person to write good stories about the Navy under attack. I happened to be around."

"Good stories," cried Lopez, "about those bastards trying to immolate us!"

"Not about them. More about how the crews are handling it."

"And you had the qualifications?" Verso said.

"Apparently. I am sufficiently neurotic according to my past girlfriends."

Lopez refilled Rosenthal's mug, and the others.

"Black coffee. Could anything be better?" Verso asked.

"Yes," said Lopez, "and she's on Waikiki Beach."

"Spoken like a married man," Verso joked.

We all chuckled. Even the Captain broke a smile, before asking, "Exactly, what are you supposed to do, Mr. Rosenthal?"

"I'm here to tell the Navy's side of the war, to make heroes out of you guys."

"Check me out during the next suicide raid, kid," Verso volunteered. "You won't see much of a hero when those *'meatballs'* are diving on us."

"Meatballs?

"The 'Rising Sun' painted on the Jap planes."

It began on bloody Easter Sunday, April 1st... It was April Fools Day. It was also Good Friday. It was the first day of the invasion of Okinawa and no one was fooling around. The suicide planes came out of the sun, crazy bastards, crashing into anything afloat.

> *RADAR, BRIDGE, MANY BOGIES! CONVERGING.*
> *BATTLESHIP IDAHO UNDER ATTACK...*
> *DESTROYERS PURDY, ZELLARS, CASSIN YOUNG*
> *DAMAGED.*
> *MINECRAFT LINDSEY HIT. FIRES OUT OF*
> *CONTROL*

Unfortunately, my youthful innocence and excitement got the best of him.

"That's why I'm here. To convince people back home that this battle can and must be won no matter what the kamikazes do. No matter the cost."

"Any cost, Mr. Rosenthal? Let me tell you about the cost. We've lost more ships in this stinking battle than in all the naval engagement of the war, Pacific or Atlantic. Christ, the whole Fifth Fleet, over 1500 ships, is on edge. We're out here on a limb, 350 miles from Tokyo and 7,000 miles from San Francisco."

As the Captain caught his breath, Verso continued my lesson. "Endless alerts, the possibility of a sudden, fiery death at any hour."

Lopez piped in … "Good guys are dying out here."

The Captain, breathing again, added, "Hell, the crews are so keyed up that they hears the *click* of a ship's loud speaker before it's even activated."

"The strain of waiting for the attacks is making everyone nuts," Verso pointed out. "It's killing morale."

"I didn't know."

"You still don't," the Captain said sharply.

Lopez interrupted. "We're at RPS 10."

"Where?"

Verso brought out a map indicating a number of dots, each numbered, ringing Okinawa. Each dot represented a radar picket station and one or two destroyers on station with some LSMR ships.

Verso said, "We're the early warning system. We do it with "big ears," our radar. We catch the Nips before they can surprise us. We alert the carriers. We the first ships the Japs encounter. They don't like us. The feeling is mutual. If they can, they try to knock us off."

"Where's the *Ward's* picket station?"

Verso pointed a stubby finger. "Right here, way out on a lonely perch. We're picket station #10

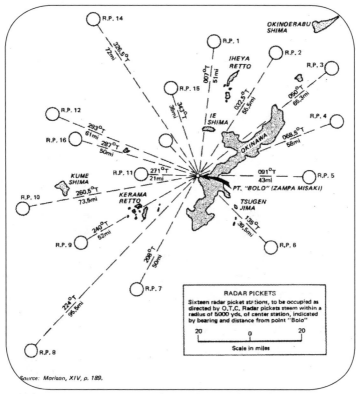

RADAR PICKET STATIONS – RPS 10 (CENTER, FAR LEFT

"Radar pickets steam within a radius of 5,000 yards of a center station, indicated by a bearing and distance from point "Bolo" off the western coast of Okinawa.

Captain Atwood brought out another map. It showed a rectangular-shaped area, which was RSP 10. Five ships were in the box. The *U.S.S. Little,* a destroyer, was in the northern section with two smaller ships. The *Ward* was in the southern section with the *195.* We patrol our box day and night in conjunction with the *U.S.S Little* and other ships.

"RPS 10 is an invisible box determined by longitude and latitude," the Captain said flatly. "This is where we patrol."

Verso followed up, saying, "We spot the Jap, then the flyboys splash him. Goodbye Rising Sun!"

"Just one problem," Lopez added. "The Jap pilots know what we're doing so they come after us --- the picket ships. We protect the fleet, but who protects us?"

"It's a mathematical equation, said the Captain. "If enough planes attack a picket ship, the early warning system will be destroyed."

Once more, Lopez interrupted. "The *Ward is* 10 degrees off the bow, sir."

"Where,"

"Over there, Mr. Rosenthal."

All faces turned toward the *Ward*, a steel, grayish warship almost hidden in the mist, approximately half-a-mile away. At first, the *Ward* was more ephemeral than substance. Seen from the smaller *195*, the destroyer was emerging huge and deadly. All gun mounts angled their guns upward toward a yet unseen prey in the western skies.

I stared at the *Ward* in disbelief. This was not the *Ward* I had seen months ago at Pearl Harbor where the ship was moored. This ship was alive, a Jules Verne creature of the seas. No longer dry-docked the *Ward* was a menacing ship-of-the-line. Disbelief turned suddenly to anxiety and then to an all-pervading fear.

"Captain, how do I get to the *Ward*?"

ATWOOD'S STORY

Captain Atwood wanted a destroyer. For him they were beautiful, flashing seals of the sea, marking 35 knots under full steam, and ready for a fight. The Navy had other ideas --- the 195. He came to love and respect the ungainly, initialized ship and the other ships with funny names --- LCSL, LCS, and LCI. All were kin to the LSMR. They fought just as bravely as the destroyers but with smaller guns --- 20 and 40mm weapons. Still, the Japs didn't enjoy the reception these ships gave them.

Captain Atwood took a special interest in RSP 10. One of 16 stations, his exact location was 260.5 degrees true, 73.5 miles from Point Bolo, the code name for the Japanese island of Zanpa Misaki just off of Okinawa. He would defend this spot to the death. That was his job, to defend and alert. And he would also make sure that Mr. Rosenthal got to the Ward.

Chapter 6

TRANSFER

I never should have asked.

I was dangling in mid-air, suspended between the *195* and the *Ward* in a Bosun's chair. The two ships were about 50 yards from each other. Dangerously, both ships were barely making headway as they tried to maintain a parallel course and speed during the transfer.

THE RIDE OF A LIFETIME

I'm sure I was ashen faced and unable to speak. Maybe scream, but not speak. I know I was excited. This was the future *Disney E-ride* of a lifetime. Someday, I thought, I'll write about this to disbelieving readers, the friendly author in a VIP chariot riding across a short and deadly expanse of water. Yes, I would write it, but not today.

From my perch I could see both ships and the sea boiling between them. Everything seem to be speaking to me --- the ropes and pulleys, the wind, the steel plates crunching on the waves, the commands of officers, and the grunting of heaving sailors on the lines. As I got closer to the *Ward*, all I could see was a wall of steel against which I might be crushed. I had a good chance, it seemed to me, to make the obituary column before writing my first story.

Finally, salvation ... I was pulled from my chair and onto the cold steel, which was the *Ward*. Maybe, I would live to write that story.

On the Bridge were Captain Brown and his Executive Officer, Bert, plus a Chief Rossi, and a yeoman, Marcus.

Quiet and self-assuming, there was no question that Captain Brown was in charge. Very much like Atwood he seemingly would be more at home behind an IRS desk than in command of a man-of-war. Bert, younger and eager for action, was tall and muscular, a former college basketball player and hero to more than one cheerleader.

The Chief was in his late thirties, a career sailor, who, as all department Chiefs will readily admit, helped the Captain run the ship. Marcus was a veteran of World War I, a reservist who was brought back post haste following Pearl Harbor. With graying hair and his mid-forty age, he was the oldest man on the ship. New recruits often confused him with the Captain.

For these three men, the bridge was their home, especially during action.

"Chief, what's the word on our journalist?" the Captain asked.

"Somewhat shaky, but surviving, He's drying off."

"Good. Let's get separated and back on patrol. I don't like being harnessed to the *195*. What's are situation, Bert?"

"The *195* is rejoining the group. She'll be in the box shadowing us, in a few minutes. Two *LCS's, 83 and 84* are in the box. They're shadowing the *U.S.S. Little*. All ships are on station and at battle alert."

"Very good."

Captain Brown looked out at the ship, first, its guns, then the gun crews in the tubs. His gaze moved to the radar masts, and finally, fell upon the ship's battle flags whipping in the wind. His eyes then turned to the largest flag, unfurled, wind-blown, cloth and color, symbolic of his country. Under his tight breath, he mumbled, "The readiness is all." His thoughts were interrupted by the appearance of his still somewhat shaken guest, one Robert Rosenthal --- that is, me.

"Mr. Rosenthal, good of you to join us," Bert remarked.

"Gentlemen."

"Enjoy the ride?" asked the Chief.

"Enjoy? I would use a different word."

Everyone laughed.

"Well, no matter, the Captain said. "You made it. We're glad to have you. It took you awhile to catch up to us."

Captain Brown was correct. Initially, I was supposed to sail with the *Ward*, but an acute appendicitis and some complications kept me in a military hospital for almost two months. Talk about bad luck.

"I wanted to sail with you, Captain."

"No matter. You're here now."

"It must have been tough with all those beautiful nurses hovering over you." the Chief suggested.

"I tried to keep up their morale."

"The Navy has high standards," Bert reflected.

"I keep that in mind next time I'm on a gurney."

There was chuckling all around, then everyone went back to business.

"Marcus, this guy will bunk with you. We've got one typewriter aboard so you'll need to share. Work out your own schedule."

"Thank you, Captain."

"I expect glowing reports about the *Ward*, Mr. Rosenthal. Glowing."

"Naturally. Lot's of personal stuff, human-interest stories, I trust. How's the grub? Do you miss your mom? Do you ever get scared? What was shore leave like?"

"Boring but acceptable," Bert said. "On the other hand, we don't want you to write too much about combat actions."

"Why not? I asked.

"When we're in one, you'll see," Bert replied.

CAPTAIN BROWN'S STORY

It was Captain Brown's job to patrol RPS 10 endlessly, day and night. He was also responsible for over 200 men, most of whom were youngsters just out of high school and growing up fast. You do that in war.

The Ward was a world of its own most noticeably at night when it became a floating fortress of steel plates pushing the cold sea aside, keeping the darkness and its demons out, protecting the men from hidden dangers, keeping them dry and safe.

In the day, his responsibility continued. The horizon widened and the sea became a vast infinity of water and sky. The ship couldn't leave the "box." It was imprisoned in an invisible jail. There was no reprieve.

The Captain often thought of the ship was a speck, a steel-plated bug swimming around in a giant lake. Around the bug, only the sun seemed to move. The Captain paid close attention to the ship's position. Recording the changing coordinates helped him to know that the ship existed, that the crew was still in the war against an implacable enemy.

The dangers were everywhere. Below, a submarine might already have sighted the Ward and loosed a torpedo. Above, a lone suicide plane, undetected by radar, might be falling from the sky already writing the Ward's obituary.

Captain Brown knew this. He could do nothing more than carry on. The ship was on station. The men were trained. All would do their duty.

Chapter 7

PERSONALITIES

FORENOON WATCH – 1100 HOUR

I stowed my gear in Marcus' compartment, which was what it was, five telephone booths thrown together to hold two bunks, one on top of the other, a wall closet, and a tiny desk just large enough for an *Underwood* with big friendly keys. At his insistence, we toured the crew's quarters. Unless you've been on a destroyer, you can't realize how crowded things are in CQ. Space is at a premium.

This was a tight little world of mattresses and hinges hanging them from steel girders, really hammocks suspended in the air. There was a small table for card players with the requisite coffee, cigarettes, and smoke in place. *Lucky Strikes*, the choice cigarette of the day, was provided free to the men courtesy of the American Tobacco Company.

Those men not in the card game tended to read. *Life Magazine* and the *Reader's Digest* were standard fare for many in addition to letters from home, which were reread numerous times.

Other men were writing home, to that someone special, a parent, girlfriend, or child. There was always someone special. As they wrote, they were aware that censors would review every word. Exactly what harm would come to the *Ward* if a five-year old knew about RPS 10, or Point Bolo was always difficult for me to understand.

Some of the crew was involved in a time-honored ritual. They were sleeping. Asleep, the terrible demands of war drifted away, and home was in your next dream. The body demanded rest and the mind desired the necessary holiday.

A collection of pre-*Playboy* girlie magazines was hidden away in lockers and duffel bags out of sight of the Captain when he inspected this area. By his own admission, he was a bit of a prude. But he was also a realist. He had a crew of hot-blooded young men, who had not yet escaped the ravages of puberty.

Three small fans provided some circulation, but never enough. Over time, your nose adjusted to the odors and smells of a cramped world in which 200 men sweating out the war. It was in the CQ that I met again a few of those men I had known back at Pearl before my body rebelled --- Warren, Willis, Granados, Wallace, and Freeman.

Marcus introduced me without unnecessary exposition. "Our journalist from San Francisco, at last."

I remembered Al Warren, who was sitting on his cot slowly rubbing linseed oil into his baseball glove. Around and around his hand worked the linseed oil into the leather mitt, darkening it and making it more pliable. He was 24-years old, my age, and built like Enos Slaughter of the St. Louis Cardinals, his hero at shortstop, and the player he would like to be. He hoped to rejoin the Hollywood Stars after the war. He was slim, tough as nails, animated, and in charge of Gun Mount 51.

He threw shells at the Nips the way he ran the bases, spikes up.

Unexpectedly, he punched his glove with a solid whack while doing an acceptable impersonation of Chick Jones, the announcer for the Stars.

He did it. Al Warren completed an almost impossible double play in the 9ᵗʰ with one out and the winning run at third. Once more, the little guy saved the day. The crowd is going crazy. The players are carrying Warren off the field. The Stars are headed for the World Series.

"World Series?" I asked. "What a story."

"For the minor leagues," he responded with a big grin. "And make sure you write all this in your reports. That's Al Warren, All-Star. Don't forget to mention the final score, one, zip."

"Shortstop of the Pacific. And who will St. Louis play?"

"The Yanks. Who else?"

"I hate the Yanks," Norm Willis bellowed.

"So does the 'bitch,' answered Warren.

All the men snickered in a sarcastic way. The "bitch" was *Tokyo Rose*, whose daily radio program warned Americans that they would die in the Pacific. This trans-planted American had one job, destroy the morale of America's fighting men by taunting them about their wives and girlfriends back home. She did this while playing music from home during her 20-minute radio broadcast each day. Her program was called the *Zero Hour*.

Her real name was less dramatic than Tokyo Rose. It was Iva Toguri, a young woman who was stranded in Japan at the outbreak of the war. After the war, though she proclaimed her innocence, she was convicted of treason and imprisoned. In 1977, President Gerald Ford pardoned her after it was proved she had been forced by the Japanese to do the broadcasts. POW's, assigned to work with her, testified on her behalf.

But in 1945, she was the "bitch."

"No way the Yanks are going to beat the Dodgers," Willis stated with total conviction. Any bets?"

Willis was standing next to his cot. He was one tough, leather-faced guy. He was a former rodeo rider before joining the Navy. He was in charge of a 40mm gun tub. He walked over to me and extended his hand. The handshake was vice-like, a test of a man's threshold for pain. I endured.

"Hi, partner," he said. "Nice to see you're up and around. That was one hell of a time to need an operation."

"Good to see you again. How's our rodeo man?"

"Corralled until this war's over. Then, it's back on the circuit. And I expect you to make me look good, even if that nasty old bull throws me. Don't give Warren all the good stuff."

"Both you and the bull will be covered."

"Did I ever tell you about the time I rode a bull for 63 seconds in Wyoming? Let me tell you…"

"Not again," cried Warren.

"I think some of the bull got into the rider," remarked Marcus.

Everyone laughed including Willis, who accepted the comment as a compliment. When things died down, Marcus introduced me to a new member of the crew, Jose Granados.

"Jose, meet Mr. Rosenthal. He's here to boost our morale."

"Greetings."

"I heard about you. Sick or something in Pearl…"

"Appendicitis.

Granados retrieved a *Bible* from his cot and held it out to me, saying, "This is my morale booster, this and a good prayer."

"I'll make sure to quote from it."

"You do that."

"Jose studied for the priesthood," Marcus interjected.

Granados was short, trim, and wiry. He's brown-skinned of Mexican heritage from the San Fernando Valley just north of Los Angeles. His family worked the rich soil for the large citrus growers. He was in charge of a damage control gang when he wasn't in the engine room.

"Almost became one, too. One more year, that's all I needed."

"After the war?" I asked.

46

"Maybe. Marcus, how come you know so much about the crew?"

"I'm a Yeoman, First Class. I read every report. I type every report. I file every report. Anything with words goes through my desk, small as it is. That's how I know everything, padre."

"Not bad for an old Jew. How old are you, pop?" Hank Wallace asked.

"Old enough to be your father."

Wallace was big, mean, and an absolute stereotype of a Southern "redneck" from the Mississippi delta area. He hated (or said he did) Negroes, Jews, and Catholics in that order. Given this, I found myself caught in the middle again, not as bad as the "blacks" or as good as the "fish eaters" to quote him out of context. Even Warren, who was from neighboring Alabama, was embarrassed by this big lug, whose unchecked mouth was almost as large as the 5-inch projectiles he helped fire.

"I remember you," I said calmly. "Wallace, right?"

"Another Jew-boy. Right, Rosenthal?"

"Guilty as charged."

"Damned Christ-killer."

There it was, the old charge, which Jews have dealt with for almost 2,000 years. Unfortunately, there was no answer, which would satisfy a Wallace.

"Not guilty of the charge," I said.

"Smart ass."

"That's what the pharaoh said to Moses. I'll make sure I quote you in my first story."

I really shouldn't have said that. It only proved that I could be a "smart ass." Wallace turned red and lumbered toward me.

Shit, I thought, two minutes on the *Ward* and I'm already under attack. Where are the Marines when you need them? Crap, I needed to get to Okinawa where it was safer

"Enough of that!"

"Who said that?

"I did, Wallace."

A new member of the crew was standing, all six-foot, five inches of him. He was holding a book, the history of something. Later, I learned his name was Abraham Freeman, a kid from South Carolina, where he had picked tobacco before being drafted.

"You talking to me, kitchen orderly? Enough of what?" Wallace asked. "Are you a Jew behind your skin?" Your name sure sounds Jewish."

"Not that it matters, but I'm a Baptist. My mother named me Abraham to honor Mr. Lincoln. Freeman is our adopted name because we're free."

Pointing to his book, Wallace said, "The boy can read. Imagine that, a 'darkie' who can read."

Freeman was visibly upset by the comment. Everyone in the CQ had seen this encounter before. They wondered if this time it would lead to blows.

"What's the matter, boy?" Wallace asked.

"Someday…"

"Someday, what?"

Before Freeman could respond, a booming voice was heard. "Save it for our little yellow friends."

Standing in the doorway was Chief Rossi looking very unhappy. Still agile for his age, he stepped between Freeman and Wallace, both of whom towered over him. He pushed each aside. Command and rank had their place.

"Damn thing, mixing us with them," Wallace commented in a fury.

"Stow it," the Chief said. "Dumb bastards, the entire Jap nation wants to blow us to hell, and you two jerks from the South are fighting with each other. Save it for after the war."

"Things will change after the war," Freeman said with conviction.

"Don't bet on it," Wallace spit back.

Trying to switch topics, I said, "Padre, what makes for a good prayer? I might need to make a couple tonight."

"Padre...I like the sound of that. Please refer to me that way in your writing. As for your question, it depends on what you're praying for."

Warren jumped in on that one. "Winning the World Series with a timely single in the 9th with two outs. Now that's a prayer come true."

"Nothing else? I asked with a smile.

"Well sure. A good-looking gal meets me after the game to celebrate. How about you, Norm?"

"Listen you guys, there would be a cute little cowgirl in the stands watching me stay on a bronco for seven seconds and first place money. That's my prayer. What about you, Freeman?"

"Returning to a new South Carolina."

"Wallace?" the Padre asked.

"Keeping Mississippi the way it was for a hundred years."

"What about you, Rosenthal?"

"Writing the great American war novel."

"Include all of us," the Padre said.

"Absolutely."

The Chief asked, "Where's Schroeder?"

"Over there in his bunk," replied Willis. Laverne can sleep through anything."

I glanced at the kid. He was asleep face up, almost angelic in appearance, a youth at sea for the first time. On his chest was a copy of Walt Whitman's *Leaves of Grass*. He was dressed in a white tee shirt and Navy shorts, standard off duty garb.

On a shelf next to him was a picture of his family. He was standing with his family in front of their house outside of Elgin, Illinois. Wearing his Navy uniform, he was young, proud, and invulnerable.

As I looked at the picture, I made a mental note: *They came from all over America, young kids to do the dirty job of war.*

"His mother sent him that book," Granados said. " Poetry. She likes poetry. He's been trying to read it since we left San Francisco."

"Never much for that stuff," the Chief spouted.

I said, "He looks so young."

"Folks signed for him. He won't be eighteen for a few more weeks," Marcus commented.

"Damn, you do know everything," Willis snapped.

"It's in his file."

"When we get back to Pearl, let's introduce him to some ladies I know," Wallace said with a snicker.

Though Wallace a bigot, he was right about one thing. Booze and women did great things for morale if you were so disposed.

At that moment, Danny woke up and lurched from his cot as if shot from a cannon. As he did, his book fell to the floor. Freeman picked it up.

"Good book, kid. Keep reading it," he said.

Granados added, "Danny, if you had one prayer answered, what would it be?"

"One prayer? I'd like to understand these poems. It would make my mother happy."

I looked closely at him. He was the "*kid next door,*" bushy-tailed, god-fearing, polite, and a hard worker. You wouldn't mind your daughter going out with him. He's finishing his high school studies in the Navy. A diploma awaited him if he could survive the Jap curriculum here off of Okinawa.

Glancing around the CQ. I realized my own prayer had already been answered. All these men --- all these stories.

SOME OF THE CREW, U.S.S. AARON WARD

GRANADOS' STORY

Jose was the damage control office on the Ward. Originally, his family came from a village south of Mexico City. His father, Miguel, crossed the U.S border via a "wetback passport." In time he married an American girl, Juanita Chavez, in Santa Fe.

Within five years, his family included four kids living in a country, which gave them a chance for a better life, a job, an education, and food on the table. He never looked back

What does a damage control gang do? It's simple. Jose trained his men to control the damage, whether from a submarine or a suicide plane. The bet is the ship will be hit by something. There will be an explosion, and metal will be ripped and torn, fires will break out, men will be trapped below deck, and it will be up to the damage control gangs to limit death's walk.

Traditional weapons will not be used in this struggle. Crowbars, battleaxes, metal cutting tools, fire hoses, battle lanterns, and hard hats compose the gang's arsenal. If the gang does its job right, the fuel tanks won't explode, nor will the ammo room ignite. Doomed men trapped below in rising cold water will be saved to fight another day.

Jose enjoyed being called padre. In truth, he hoped to complete his clerical training after the war. He wanted to do damage control for God.

Chapter 8

COLD STORAGE

I continued my impromptu tour of the *Ward* with Chief Rossi. We sought out Doc Ferrell's lair. We were walking down a long corridor, which had closed compartment doors on either side. It was a sealed world of hidden rooms.

"Thanks, Chief. I really appreciate the tour. You know, getting reacquainted with the ship."

"No problem. I wouldn't want you to confuse the bow with the stern in your writing."

"In other words, don't get things ass backward."

"As you say."

"One thing, Chief. Why are we here? Why not look for the doctor in the dispensary?

"Doc Ferrell isn't there at this time of the day. He's here, checking."

"Checking?"

On cue, Doc Ferrell stepped out of one the compartments. He left the door partially ajar.

He was wearing a heavy Navy pea coat and his collar was up. He also had on gloves and a heavy woolen beanie. As always, his moustache was trimmed and there was a twinkle in his eyes.

"Well, well, Mr. Rosenthal. I heard you were aboard, or at least most of you."

"I left 'you know what' in Pearl."

"Good as any place, I suppose."

"Blasted thing."

"Sorry I had to give you the bad news. I know you really wanted to stay on the *Ward*, but it was better to do the operation in Honolulu."

Before I could respond, the Chief jumped into the conversation. "The Captain wants him to see what the medical profession is doing for the ship's morale."

"Does he now?"

"Yes."

"Okay Mr. Reporter. But one thing…"

"Yes."

"Make sure you spell my name right in your articles --- two *R's, 2 L's.*"

"No problem."

"Chief, get this fellow a jacket and the rest."

The Chief grabbed two pea coats from a cabinet by the door and two pairs of gloves. They were similar to what Doc Ferrell was wearing.

"Put this on," he instructed. "It's colder than a bare ass in the middle of winter in there."

"What is this room," I asked.

"We call it the Cold Storage Room," Doctor Ferrell said.

The three men entered the room, which was much larger than I would have thought. The refrigerated room stored meats and vegetables, fruit, whatever needed a low temperature. Inside the room was another sailor, dressed as we were. He was bent over with a notebook and pencil in his hands. He was counting plastic bags of something carefully placed in strong cardboard boxes. He saw us and stood up. The man was tall, dignified, and athletic. And he was an Apache.

"Little Bear, it's time to meet our guest."

"Mr. Rosenthal? Right?"

"I'll confess to that name."

"I never forget a case. A ruptured appendix, I believe."

"How can my appendix be so famous? I asked a bit frustrated.

"Beats me," he said.

"What are you doing?" I asked.

"Bookkeeping."

Doctor Ferrell moved to Little Bear's open box and pulled out a plastic bag, which he handed to me.

Chief Rossi said, "Doc here has plasma stored all over the ship, wherever there's refrigeration. He figures the Nips might get lucky and knock out his office. Might get his plasma. He won't let that happen."

"There's life in these bags, Mr. Rosenthal, Little Bear said. Every donor is here in this room, in this box. Every state…"

"Who knows, could be the blood in this bag came from a mechanic in Detroit a housewife in Florida, or Lord help us, a politician in Washington," Doc Ferrell pointed out.

"As long as it doesn't come from a Negro in Mississippi," Little Bear said. "For a few guys that's a medical sin."

"What?" I asked.

"Mississippi has a stupid law. No mixing blood between the races under any circumstances. As if a wounded sailor out here would care."

"Or even know," added the Chief.

"Would Wallace care? I asked.

"He would." Marcus said.

"Ask Doc about the ice cream machine, Mr. Rosenthal," the Chief urged.

"O.K., what about the ice cream machine?"

"Most destroyers don't have one," Doctor Ferrell said.

"But the *Ward* does?"

"You bet," said the Chief. "Bolted against the forward bulkhead of the crew's mess hall. And it's loaded with blood plasma."

"Tell him about the allowance, Doc."

"You really want me to, Chief?"

"Of course."

A strange glow crept over Doctor Ferrell's face and the twinkle in his eyes seemed to get larger.

"Well, it's like this. A destroyer's usual plasma allowance is 25 bags of plasma, certainly no more than 50. But we have over 250 units stored all over the ship."

"How…?"

"I comforted the men."

"You what?"

Little Bear took over, explaining to me what happened.

"Doc explained to the crew before we left Pearl that blood donors were entitled to a shot of whiskey if they needed it for medical purposes. Perhaps a second shot if they were in need. It turned out that, following their donation, most of the crew needed comforting. You never saw so many men who were near fainting, growing paler by the minute, or short of breath. It was a regular epidemic. Hell, some of the men wanted to give more than one donation. I guess they needed a lot of comforting."

The Chief provided us with his two cents at this point. "Doc is stingy with the plasma. He tells everyone he wants to return to Pearl with his allotment unused. Can you imagine that? What a spoil sport."

"Doesn't seem right," I said.

"Damn right," the doctor replied. "Damn right."

No one had to ask why Doc Ferrell was so stingy. Some things are all too obvious.

"Mr. Rosenthal," he said.

"Yes?"

"Get a word in about Little Bear. He was in graduate school before the war at New Mexico State. Pre-med student. In its wisdom, the Navy made him an orderly in the kitchen. With the Captain's blessing, I made him my assistant. He's the best medic n the fleet."

DOC FERRELL' STORY

Doc was the medical officer aboard the ship, a one-man clinic using the mess hall as a hospital, if necessary. Before the war, he worked at San Francisco General Hospital. Most of his patients were poor. They couldn't afford private medicine. When the war came, he figured he'd continue helping the poor, the poor bastards who were drafted into the service. He'd been doing it now for three years, first on the U.S.S. Saufley, DD 465, and now on the Ward.

He was real busy on the Saufley --- all over Guadalcanal and the Solomon Islands, and later the Philippines. It was a good ship with a fine crew. Unfortunately, he did need his plasma bags on the Saufley. That's when he learned his lesson. Always carry more than you'll ever hope to use.

Doc Ferrell was originally from Kentucky, born and raised in a border state before moving to California after getting his medical degree from U.K. His folks had drifted into horse country from North Carolina, and their folks had fought in the Civil War. You can guess on what side.

He grew up in a Jim Crow state, where laws, rituals, and practices discriminated against Negroes in schools, swimming pools, and in the job market. His folks accepted the situation, though on a personal level, they treated everyone with respect, and taught him to do so. The problem was, as they pointed out to him, you had to live with your neighbors who fully supported the notion of "separate but equal" in the public schools and housing.

Doc Ferrell knew things would have to change after the war. Guys like Wallace would have to change. The whole South would have to change. Otherwise, what was this war about? Survival alone? Nothing else?

He hoped to see Little Bear become a doctor. He'd be a good one. He knew the crew would find this out if the bad guys attacked the Ward.

Doc Ferrell was almost fifty. He wanted to live long enough to see the changes he envisioned.

Every man needs a dream.

Chapter 9

THE OIL KING

AFTERNOON WATCH - 1200 HOUR

The Chief handed me off to the Executive Officer, Bert. He had a first name, Howard, but he never used it. It was Bert, or Mr. Bert, possibly Officer Bert, but never Howard. He was second in command to Captain Brown.

"I'll be your guide for awhile. The Chief was needed elsewhere."
"Fine."
"How's the tour going?"
"Great."
"Any stories?"
"Everywhere I look."
"Good."
"One question, though."
"Shoot."
"We seem to be following that guy. Why?"
"Keen eye, Mr. Rosenthal."
"And?"

Bert didn't answer my question. We continued to follow a little guy, who slid around the ship like a shadow, first here, then there, always on the move above and below the deck. He carried a flashlight, a dirty rag, a steel tape measure, and a clipboard.

We watched him remove little brass plates from the deck, then place his steel tape into a small hole.

"What's he doing? I asked.
"He's the oil king."
"What's that?"
"He's the one guy we can't do without. Ever."
"Because?"
"He keeps a careful measurement of the oil in the *Ward's* tanks. Based on his inventory, the Captain can estimate the ship's fuel supply and how far the ship can steam at different speeds."
"No one gauge?"
"Exactly."
"Important job. The crew must like him."
"Depends."

Bert smiled. I was so innocent, at least for the moment.

"The problem is he's an intruder with greasy hands. By necessity, he's got to climb into every nook and cranny to measure our bunker fuel, and he's got the Captain's permission to do so. He'll walk across freshly swabbed decks or prowl around the men when they're trying to take a nap or keep a crap game going. He's been known to leave finger prints on clean bulkheads."

This was a guy you couldn't live with or without, I thought.

"He's got a name?"
"Slick Lott."
"You're kidding."
"No. The crew stuck him with it. Makes sense, doesn't it" Oil is slick and we need a lot of it."

"His real name?"

"Herbert Johnson from St. Paul. Worked in a gas station before all this."

"Looks like he still is," I commented.

"Let's head for the engine room."

Bert directed me toward the forward engine room, where we met Boxer Jernigan, the Chief of this area.

Boxer was amply named. Seven years as a professional fighter, light-heavy weight division, plus numerous altercations in Honolulu bars, had earned him the right to his name. He was built like a fire hydrant, and was one tough hombre.

"Boxer, you remember Mr. Rosenthal?"

"Kid with the gut ache? Sure. How you doing sonny?"

Sonny. No one calls me sonny. But on second thought, considering Boxer's brawn, I might make an exception.

"On the mend. Good to see you again."

"Touring with Bert?"

"Yes."

"Permit me to blow my own whistle. I'm the guy, along with my crew, who turns oil into steam, and steam is power. No steam, the *Ward* sits unless the Captain wants the crew to row."

"Consider me a novice, but how does all this work?"

"Simple," Boxer responded, "the engineers keep fire under the boilers to create super-heated steam; the steam drives the turbines, which generate electricity, and that magic powers everything on the *Ward*, including the guns.

For the first time, I took a good look at the engine room. It was a maze of dials and meters, pipes and valves, handles and wrenches. Next to it was the forward fire room. Here and there were the furnaces, which drove the engines. It was hot and sticky here, a place where men sweated and cussed, and powered the ship.

Boxer was right. Everything depended on the steam generating electricity to steer the *Ward* evasively in the event of a hot running torpedo or an explosive egg falling from the sky. This is where the power came from to run the three 5-inch gun mounts and to extend the guns skyward. Power from the engine room run the pumps to put out fires, or to suck water overboard when the ship was flooded. The radar, the eyes of the *Ward,* worked because of power generated deep within the ship.

Boxer showed a bit of his competitiveness and engine room pride, "Don't get me wrong, the Oil King is an important guy, but he doesn't turn a gallon of it into power. I do that."

"I'll remember that."

"Remember this, too. If the ship is hit, the last guys to know what's happening work in this room. If we have abandon ship, the last guys out will be covered with grease and oil. The Captain depends on us to keep the lights on for as long as possible."

"Got it."

"Good. One other thing, our motto down here."

"Which is?"

"More steam, men, more steam."

'We need to talk more," I said.

"We will."

Bert led me to our final destination. As we walked, he said, "Make sure you ask him about his doughnuts and the crapper."

"You're kidding?"

"Great story, but you may have to run for your life after he tells it."

"I'll keep that in mind."

We proceeded deeper into the bowels of the ship. I noticed that Bert was a little uneasy.

"Anything wrong?"

"Not really. I always get a little jumpy when I go the *Ward's* magazine room."

"We're not talking a library reading room."

Bert laughed and said, "I'll assume you're making a joke. No, we're almost there, directly under the crew's quarters. This is where we store tons of high explosives, the ammunition, enough here to blow us out of the water if we caught a direct hit. It happened to the *Mount Hood*, a supply ship. The ship and the crew just disappeared."

"Christ."

"When we got to the magazine room, Bert checked me for matches, a lighter, anything that could spark, including heel plates on my shoes.

"This is really necessary," I asked.

"The gods in this room sleep lightly. We don't want to wake them."

"Agreed."

Two weapon carrying Marines checked us before we entered the magazine. Only then did I gaze at this alien landscape.

It was like nothing I had ever seen before. I felt like I was in an Egyptian tomb. It was dark, cool, and deadly quite.

Everywhere there were powder cans in their racks in neat rows higher than a man's head, hundreds of them. The cans were silent and inert. But one shouldn't be fooled. Wrapped within them was a potentially raging giant waiting for any tiny spark to arouse him.

I felt the hairs on the back of my neck crawling away from my skin. Bert noticed my uneasiness.

"Don't worry about it. Everyone feels this way when they enter this room the first time."

"You, too?"

"I calm myself by remembering two old Navy jokes."

"I could use a joke."

Bert smiled and explained what a tough old Gunnery Chief once told him. "You goof off in the magazine just once, by God, and it'll be the last time you ever do."

"Some joke."

"But true."

"The other joke?"

"A man who lights a match in the magazine can be put on report for leaving the ship without permission."

I couldn't help myself. I grinned.

"See. You're calmer already," Bert pointed out.

"I'm too frightened to be scared," I explained.

"Nice turn of the words."

Something caught my eye.

"What kind of shells are those? They look strange."

"Something the Japs never dreamed about --- a VT-fused, radio-proximity shell, our newest weapon, a secret one. You can't write about it."

"O.K., after the war when McArthur kicks the Emperor in the ass. How does it work?"

"Each VT shell carries a miniature radio set in its nose which is activated when it is shot out of a gun. The VT doesn't have to directly hit an enemy aircraft. It just needs to get close enough to let the electronic wizard in its nose work. The shell explodes when it gets close to a kamikaze."

"That's something."

"Makes life miserable for the Jap pilots."

"That's an edge, the VT's."

"Believe me, we need it."

BOXER'S STORY

He was born in 1913 in Newark. He joined the Navy in '38. He thought the Navy would be easier than boxing. He was a plank-owner; that is, an original member of the Ward's crew.

Boxer had many stories to tell and a wisdom born of serving on a fighting ship. He liked to talk about sweat.

As he told me, everyone sweats during combat. Combat sweat, he argued, has an odor much stronger than regular sweat. It's the sweat of impending death. It's the sweat brought about by a suicide plane diving on your ship.

The ship sweats, too, especially when maneuvering at high speed with all the guns firing. It's like the ship is alive and scared along with the crew.

Sweat was an important part of Boxer's philosophy of life.

Men die in war. Men are buried in wartime, but how do you bury someone at sea?" First, the guy is in luck. He no longer sweats. But he still needs to be buried. Canvas is cut to his size and sewn shut at the bottom. After placing the lucky jerk in it, two 5-inch shells are put inside the canvas to make the body sink. The boatswain sews up the body and shells. Next stop is the fantail where a prayer is said, taps are played, and a gun salute is completed. The body is on a board covered with an American flag. The board is lifted and the body falls feet first into the sea. The flag stays on the board.

Even the toughest guys brave a few tears as the bag falls into a bottomless deep. Burial at sea is a sad ritual, brutal, beautiful, and final.

Afterwards, the crew goes back to sweating.

Part III

UNDER ATTACK

I have not yet begun to fight.

John Paul Jones

Don't give up the ship.

Captain James Lawrence

It follows then as certain as that night succeeds the day, that without a decisive naval force we can do nothing definitive, and with it, everything honorable and glorious.

President George Washington

Chapter 10

THE ONE-MINUTE RULE

<AFTERNOON WATCH – 1300 HOUR>

AFTERNOON WATCH – 1300 HOUR

I was hungry. It was 1:00 p.m. and my stomach's 24-hour clock was rebelling. I needed fuel.

Bert dropped me off at the mess hall, where I indulged in "mystery stew," a thick slice of dark bread, a triangle of apple pie, and two cups of very black coffee. It was wonderful.

At Bart's request, Al Warren escorted me for the next part of my tour. He was a good choice. I was going to learn about the *Ward's* guns.

Warren took me directly to the forward 5-inch gun mount. He explained that there were four such mounts on the ship with two guns per mount. The barrels of the forward mount were elevated, as were the others. All guns were assigned their own sector of the sky.

Though radar could locate an enemy plane miles away, lookouts were limited to about a 5-mile visual range.

Warren explained the deadly mathematics of combat. The *Ward's* big guns had about one-minute to put up a curtain of fire, to smash the suicide plane and to save the ship once a plane entered the five-mile space around the ship.

One minute to fill the sky with hot metal and sting a bat.

"See these guns, Rosenthal," Warren said, "these are our big ones, the 5-inch, 38 cal. guns."
"How far will they shoot?"
"How far and how accurately, you mean?"
"Yes."
"Basic law of physics… Eleven pounds of explosives generate enough energy to hurl a fifty-four pound projective about nine miles."
"That far! I didn't realize one guy's finger on the trigger could do that."
"One guy! Are you kidding? It takes at least twenty-five men to operate a mount."

I was astounded. It never occurred to me that so many people were involved. I was still learning. There had to be good stories here.

"That many…"
"Let me explain it to you. You need to get it right in your reports."
"Explain away."

Warren took a big breath and then dove into the subject.

"Twenty-five guys, and each with a specific job. First, there's the *mount captain*, who communicates by phone with the *gun control officer*. He s assisted by the *pointer,* who controls the guns in a vertical plane. The *trainer* is responsible for moving the guns in a horizontal plane. Then there is the *sight-setter*, who makes slight adjustments for wind and range when the gun is fired by local control. Finally, there's the *fuse-setter* who makes sure the shells explode at a predetermined time, unless we're using the VT's."
"Just to fire one shell. Damn."

Catching another breath, Warren continued. He was really into it now.

"This is just the beginning. Nothing would happen if it wasn't for the guys doing the physical work."

"What work?"

"The hot, sweaty work. *The projectile-loaders* who slam the shells into the open breeches; the *powder-loaders* who heave big powder cans in after the shells; *the spade-men* who check that the breech is close, and the *hot-shell* men who wear asbestos gloves."

"Why gloves?"

"They snatch out the smoking powder cases and heave them out the mount's chute onto the deck."

I realized you don't throw things in the Navy. You heave them. You don't eat. You chow. You don't sleep. You bunk.

"The real story is below deck," Warren continued. "Below the gun mount is the upper handing room. Nine to twelve men work in there. They have one job --- keep the ammunition going up the electric hydraulic hoists. Below them is the magazine room. The guys in there move the projectiles out of storage racks. It's a tough, dirty job."

I was impressed and confused. With all those men necessary to fire one salvo, how fast could the guns fire? I asked Warren this question.

"A well-drilled crew can spit out as many as thirty shells per minute."

"Thirty!"

I was really impressed. I guess my face showed it.

"That's why the Navy drills, and drills, and drills, but we're never fast enough if a Nip breaks through our fire."

Warren now confessed to me that he was something of a tyrant. He needed to be, he pointed out. He was in charge of gun mount 51.

"I push the guys hard. Within our steel shell, which was riveted to the *Ward's* deck, was life and death; death for the Jap pilots and life for our crew if my men did their work right. There was no room for error. In the dead air and stifling heat of our enclosure, with the ship heaving and rolling in the seas, we danced to a lethal ballet."

Warren accepted only one ancient reply from his crew, which harkened back to John Paul Jones.

"CONTROL ... MOUNT 51, MANNED AND READY."

WARREN' STORY

Warren wanted to continue in professional baseball when he was done with shooting planes out of the sky. He loved the game.

The pitcher throws a mile-high curve ball and Warren slugs a line drive to the centerfield wall. An imposing hitter for the other side whacks the cowhide to deep short, a sure hit, but Warren catches up to it with a sliding catch in the dust.. The first base coach tells him to steal second base. He does it, spikes up. The third base coach orders him to head for third as the hitter lays down a bunt along the first base line. He crashes into third base face down in the dirt. A hit later, he scores the winning run.

The crowd roars, the flash bulbs pop. The game is over.

Out here in the South China Sea at RPS 10 there were no bleacher seats for the working fans, or box seats for the well heeled. There were no crowds pouring into the ballpark. There were no overweight umpires, thin program sellers in your face, or loud hotdog vendors. There was no scoreboard in centerfield to tell Warren who was ahead.

But one thing was the same. Al Warren wanted to win. This was his game of the year, each day he played. When the score was tallied, he wanted to know only one thing. Would he play again tomorrow? Would the season continued?

Was there a chance for the World Series, which, in his mind, meant everything in the world.

He liked to say that on the Ward, Captain Brown was the manager. He kept the team together. The Executive Officer carried out the Captain's wishes. That was Bert's role. He pushed the coaches, who pushed the men, who pushed the enemy. Along the way, there was a lot of yelling and growling, and language that brought a reddish tinge to the Captain's cheek, along with a satisfied feeling.

In the gun mounts, Warren's players, hidden from the fans by a wall of steel, did their jobs in bleak light. If they caught a runner off base, they wouldn't see it. If a fast moving player for the opposing side headed for home plate, they wouldn't know it. If the other side scored, Warren's guys wouldn't know it until it happened.

Warren's teammates depended on their skill --- on their guns --- and their officers to get them through nine innings. That meant sending the kamikaze pilots to their ancestors.

5-INCH GUN TURRET

Chapter 11

THE THREE STRIKE RULE

—————————————

Chief Rossi found us and took over for Warren.

"Follow me to the small guns," he said. "Time to meet the mighty mites, or as some would say, our last defense."

We walked a few feet.

"Over there," he said, pointing at the gun tubs for the 20 and 40 mm guns.

I looked. Gun tub was an accurate description. Imagine your bathtub, somewhat larger and three or four men in it with their gun and ammo. That about covered it.

"You know," he said, the men in the mounts shoot and shoot, but they never really see what they're shooting at. Radar and fire control command them, and walls encase them. They're not blind; they just can't see the outside world. But these fellows in the tubs… They can see everything!"

"Maybe it's better that way. Who wants to see a suicide plane coming right at you?"

Point well taken… Of course, it really doesn't matter whether you can see them. The three-strike rule is always in effect."

"What?"

"Put this into your notes. The Navy's been out here since April 1ˢᵗ and so have the Japs. Over a hundred ships have been hit so far: battleships, cruisers, carriers, and destroyers. The Navy classified the "hits" to bring order to the chaos. There are three categories.

"Categories?"

"We refer to them as strikes. Lightly damaged ships are patched up and sent back to duty fast."

"The others?"

"Strike two is a stateside hit. The damage can't be fixed easily. You need to get back to Pearl, Seattle, or Mare Island near San Francisco. Not a bad deal if the crew doesn't have to pay too high a price."

"Severe damage doesn't occur without casualties."

"Exactly."

I thought about the third category. It could only be one thing. I hesitated to ask the Chief.

"Sailors caught in a third strike are at the bottom of the sea."

I digested that information and realized that Chief Rossi might have faced all three pitches. As a reporter, I wanted to know more. But I was embarrassed to ask.

"No need to be shy, Mr. Rosenthal. You're here to tell a story. I'm here to give you a few chapters."

He gathered himself before speaking. When he did, he spoke for himself and old shipmates now plying other seas or swallowed by them.

"Back in '43 during the Guadalcanal campaign, I was on the second ship named for old Admiral Aaron Ward --- the *U.S.S. Aaron Ward, DD 483.*"

"Second *Ward*?"

"You're on the third *Ward*."

To say I was confused would be an under statement. Three *Wards!*! How could that be?

The Chief read my face and smiled.

"Don't worry, I'll fill you in. Let's talk about the second *Ward*. The ship got caught in Iron Bottom Strait off Guadalcanal. We took three direct hits from Jap cruisers and met Davey Jones that day. I was lucky. I was blown off the ship into shallow, warm waters without a scratch. Can you believe it? Other guys weren't so lucky."

My extended college education limited me to one word. "Wow!"

"The Navy decided to build another *Ward*. You're on it, the *DM 40*."
"*DM*?"
"Destroyer minelayer."
"What about the first *Ward*?"
"Later

The Chief brought me down to two tubs, two twin 40's and quad 40's. Except for lightweight splinter shield, the gunners were completely out in the open and vulnerable. He showed me how the ammo came up from the clipping rooms below the forties.

"When you hear the 40's, "he said with a smirk, "you can bet the kamikazes have evaded the 5-inchers and they are closing fast."
"And when you hear the 20's?"
"Son, we've got eight 20mm guns around the ship. They're the last line of defense. If you hear the 20's, say your prayers."

I looked at the three-man teams operating the 20mm guns. As the Chief had said, they were last line of defense with hell descending upon them. Privately, I hoped they were good shots.

"See that kid over there in the 20's tub? That's Laverne Schroeder. We all look after him, some as a brother, others as a father. Doesn't even shave yet, but can he shoot that gun. All of us older guys depend on that kid to shoot straight."

I couldn't help but wonder, what brought a farm kid to this place?

LAVERNE'S STORY

His dad had a small farm outside of Elgin. They grew corn mainly and raised about 50 milk cows, a few pigs, and lots of chickens. His mother taught school, the third grade. Two brothers and a sister filled out the family. Uncles and aunts dotted the Illinois landscape, plus a few acres in Indiana.

His dad was a Bible reader, but not much more. Danny's mother was a Quaker, but didn't push it. The kids were taught to believe in God, respect the law, and try not to hurt anyone. Not bad advice. His dad read the local newspaper religiously. His mother read poetry.

The whole family worked hard, especially during the Depression. Farm prices were down. It was difficult to make money.

Danny was a sophomore in high school when the war broke out. His older brother, Jacob, joined the Marines. For all Danny knew, he might have been on Okinawa. In his senior year, he convinced his parents to let him join the Navy. It wasn't an easy sell. His mother, especially, was against it. Danny's argument finally won her over. He couldn't stay home while his friends enlisted or were drafted. He felt uncomfortable being young, strong, and in school.

One really good friend, Brenda, was sad to see him enlist. I guess they were in love, whatever that means at 17-years of age. They promised to write to each other.

The Navy discovered that he had excellent eyesight and sent him to gunnery school. All that deer and fox hunting with his dad and brothers paid off. Pretty soon he was training on the 20's and earning high marks. It seemed he could lead a target right into his tracers. The Navy called him a "natural."

From all I could learn, Danny really didn't like the idea of killing someone, but that was what Uncle Sam was paying him to do. In his gun tub, he spat out death at anything, which moved in the sky with a meatball on it. But somehow, it didn't seem right. His mother's Quaker philosophy had influenced him.

On the other hand, he had buddies all over the ship, mostly young guys like himself, all hardly out of high school, and still waiting for enough facial hair to shave for the first time. They didn't want to die from an exploding suicide plan. They wanted to catch a baseball game, or go to the latest movie, or prepare for a job interview --- and, eventually, meet that special girl and marry. It was Danny's job to make sure they could. Quakerism could only extend so far.

He was looking forward to next week. He would turn 18 and he knew the guys were planning something. No girls, just a big cake and lots of teasing with the Captain officiating. His mother had sent him a birthday card and a book. She urged him to read it and to think kindly about those he must fight.

He wanted to read it before the war was over.

Chapter 12

BOGIES

AFTERNOON WATCH – 1400 HOUR

I met up with Murray Lansing in the Radar Room. He would become in time my best friend on the *Ward* and for long after the war.

The room was crowded. Men peered intently into a world of MK XII and MK III radarscopes used for surface and air search. The dim ceiling lights and the phosphorus greenish glow of the scopes created an eerie world of men and machines.

Other men were at plotting boards, pencils and chalk marking the latest position of all friendly ships and planes, and, if they came, enemy forces. Others were on phones to the bridge, providing the Captain with the latest information or to Fire Control. Some were on the TBS *(Talk Between Ships)* phones. Usually, this was with the destroyer *U.S.S. Little* and the *195*.

The Radar Room Commander was Murray. His aide was Kenneth Kang, a Japanese/Chinese-American from Bakersfield in the central valley of California. As to his unusual name, that happens when your mother is Japanese and your father is Chinese. The young man was the splitting image of Gary Cooper if only he had been taller. He was, however, lanky and taciturn.

At the moment, Lansing was speaking with the Captain by phone.

"Right. Many bogies. Very faint, sir… Converging from the west. I'll keep you posted."

I gazed at the plotting board. The bogies were marked: the approximate number, speed, distance, and direction of the bogies was noted. The board left little doubt. Something was coming toward them. Something was headed for the *Ward*. The men at the board exchanged knowing looks.

Speaking to no one in particular, Kang said, "Maybe they'll turn."

On the bridge, men and officers are going about their duties. Captain Brown was absorbed in his own thoughts. Why today? Tomorrow would be better. The Captain posed the questions knowing full well they had no good answers. It was just a little game he played to maintain his outward cool.

He shifted his gaze to a display case riveted to a steel wall of the bridge. The case housed a sword. Not just any sword, but the one worn by Admiral Aaron Ward during the Spanish-American War (1898) when he showed gallantry in Manila Bay against the Spaniards. In appreciation the Navy would eventually name three destroyers after him.

That was his kind of war, the Captain thought. Ship against ship, gun against gun, salvo against salvo, men against men who want to live, not suicide pilots and planes seeking immortality.

I wandered in during the Captain's meditations.

"Captain."
"Mr. Rosenthal. Enjoying the tour?"

"Very much so."

"Good. Are you ready for another story? We just might have one for you today."

"Always. After all, I'm the ship's spinner of yarns.

The Captain spoke to Bert.

"We've got *bats* coming our way."
"How many?"
"At least fifteen."
"Christ."

I interjected. "Bats are coming are way?"
"Our little Tokyo friends seem intent upon immolating themselves on our decks today."

Back in the Radar Room tension had increased. If humanly possible, even the machines were jumpy. Something was happening out there to the west.

"Faint contacts, sir, at the extreme distance of our radar," Lansing said on the phone, "blurred images on the screens. Recommend holding off on going to *General Quarters*"

Lansing put down the phone and spoke quietly to Kang. "God, I hope I made the right decision."

"Perhaps our friends have a new type of plane," Kang responded.
"What?"
"You know, like the balloons we've heard about."

The Japanese had attached a light incendiary explosive to hundreds of balloons and released them in the mid-Pacific. The hoped the winds would carry them to the forests of the Pacific coasts, where they might set forest fires."

"Balloons would be nice today," Lansing declared.

"A nice rice bowl and seasoned fish would be better

"Food, at a time like this?"

"Okay, just sushi.

The small talk calmed the room.

A radioman interrupted them. "Damn. They're turning. Bogies. Bearing 235. Distance 45 miles."

"Confirmed," said a second radioman.

""What's up?" asked Captain Brown. "Give it to me straight, Lansing."

The Captain listened for a moment, then put down his phone.

"The bats are loose," he said to everyone on the bridge. We're going to have visitors. *Sound General Quarters."*

Throughout the *Ward* men stopped what they were doing and hustled to their assigned battle stations.

- Engine Room – Boxer Jernigan
- Mess Hall – Doc Ferrell and Little Bear
- Damage Control – Jose Granados
- Handling Room – Wallace
- Gun Turret 52 – Warner
- 40mm Tub – Willis
- 20mm Tub – Laverne Schroeder
- Radar Room – Lansing and Kang
- Bridge – Captain Brown
- Bridge – Bert
- Bridge – Chief Marcus
- Engine Room – Jernigan
- Damage Control – Slick Lott
- Mess Hall – Abraham Freeman

Chapter 13

THE READINESS

———————————

I could only watch as the *Ward* prepared for battle.

I heard the claxons blaring, sending a strident bellowing throughout the ship. This was the Navy's traditional alarm to all hands. An unseen voice echoed the ancient cry of ships in harm's way: *"Man your battle stations."*

Everywhere on the ship sailors were responding to the metallic cry of General Quarters.

Men wearing only shorts were drawn from their sleep. In a frenzy of motion, they grabbed for pants, shirts, and shoes. Others leaped from card tables, men running in one direction, cards flying in another. Letters, books, and magazines were forgotten as men headed to their battle stations.

Wallace threw down what looked like a winning card hand and headed for Mount 51, uttering a one-word editorial, "Shit."

Had Danny been in his bunk and, prompted into action by the incessant clanging of alarm bells, he would have leaped from his cot and run for his gun tub. As fate would have it he was already at his station.

Granados tucked his *Bible* inside his shirt. In one practiced movement, he opened a locker and pulled out his work uniform --- a fire fighting jacket, pants, thick boots, and leather gloves. He glanced upward for a movement and said a silent prayer before hurrying to his damage control station.

Little Bear stopped stowing pots and pans. He moved to the mess room and began preparing for the inevitable. From storage drawers he pulled out the other tools of his trade --- bandages, morphine, and plasma bags. He would be ready for Doc Ferrell.

Warren placed his beloved fielders glove under his pillow, and muttered to himself as he moved to his station, "I hope this game is rained out."

Willis had been looking at a photograph of himself atop a giant bull in some long ago rodeo. He was hanging on for his life. As he tore off for his battle station, he remarked aloud to no one in particular, "I'm still hanging on."

----------ᘓᕈᘓ----------

The bridge was alive with activity.

""Radar reports new contacts," Bert said. "Still faint. Directly from the West."

"Damn witching hours," the Chief said quietly under his breath.
"*Witching hours*? I asked.
"The time when Tokyo's bats fly," he responded.
"Usually at dawn or dusk," Bert added. "Always with the sun to their back."
"And uncertain light in your eyes?"
"Very poetic, Mr. Rosenthal, and quite correct," the Captain added.
"Mount 51 is training," Marcus said matter-of-factly.

From they're perch on the Bridge, they watched the forward gun turret turn as instructed by the fire director. Mount 51 was searching the western skies in response to the glowing radar screens. The twin 5-inch guns were at once menacing and reassuring as they sniffed the horizon and the guns elevated. Warren's voice was heard over the intercom, **"Mount 51, manned and ready."**

They couldn't see them, of course, but directly below Warren's guns, men working in a small cavity of the ship were sending projectiles and powder cases up the electric hoists to the gun mount. The were participating in an ago old Navy tradition --- "passing the ammo." Over the intercom, reassuring words were heard, **"Handling rooms, manned and ready."**

They glimpsed Norm Willis and his 40mm gun crew. They were in the tub in full battle gear: flack jackets, metal helmets, and prayers on their lips. The 40mm guns were rotating, even as Willis said, **"Forward 40's, manned and ready."**

They couldn't see Laverne Schroeder but they knew what was happening. He was in his tub rotating the 20mm guns, training them on the western horizon. His guns, as elsewhere, were ready. **"20mm guns manned and ready."**

Granados was on deck with his team of seven men. All of them were wearing their fire retardant clothing. They were prepared to for the worst: explosions, fires, and trapped sailors. **"Mid-ship repair party, manned and ready."**

"All stations, manned and ready, Captain," Bert reported.

Captain Brown nodded his approval.

Had I been flying high above the *Ward* and over RPS 10 with a God's eye view, I would have seen the ship knifing through the afternoon waters. In the distance was the *195* attempting to stay close to the destroyer. To the northeast was the *Little*, and her accompanying "small boys." Though unsaid, all ships knew, **RPS 10 was on station and manned."**

Whatever was headed eastward would receive a warm welcome. The *"readiness"* was on.

The *195* was pushing and shoving her way through the waves trying to keep within eyesight of the *Ward*.

"Christ! I thought we could get through his one day. Just once, you'd think we could have the day off," Verso said.

"Tell that to the Marines," Lopez countered.

"He's got a point," Captain Atwood shared.

There was no question about that. On shore, the Marines, who initially met light resistance when they landed, were now meeting increased resistance, then overwhelming resistance. They were fighting for their lives around the clock. The island had become a slaughterhouse for both sides, and especially for the civilians caught in the middle. The Japanese refused to lay down their arms. They wouldn't surrender. They would have to be destroyed one cave at a time, one pillbox at a time. A terrible price would be paid for this island.

"Any chance this tub can go AWOL? Lopez asked.

"Not easily," the Captain said. "Put me on TBS."

A moment later he was speaking to the *Ward*.

"*Ward, 195*. Maintaining position. Right, we'll be here to fetch you out of the water if it comes to that."

"Ask about the film," Lopez chimed.

"Another thing. Let's trade movies. We've got the Marx Brothers. We'll trade for Rita Hayward." The Captain listened for a movement before ending the connection.

"What'd they say? Lopez asked.

"They said we're the Marx Brothers, and they'll take Rita's legs over our slap happy routine."

"That's a thank you," Verso snapped.

"One other thing," the Captain announced.

"Here it comes," Lopez said.

"The bogies are closing on us."

"No way we'll see Rita tonight."

"I should have joined the Coast Guard," Verso stated.

Whatever was happening on the *Ward* was similarly occurring on the *Little*. The two "little boys" to the north were also on alert and prepared.

Aboard the *Ward* at that moment, Lansing reported to the Captain. "Bridge, Radar, many bogies. I repeat, many bogies. Bearing 235, distance 20 miles."

Chapter 14

THE ENEMY

"Follow me, Mr. Rosenthal," Mr. Rossi said with a sharpness to his voice. "Quickly."

In quick tandem we moved into the Combat Information Center, (CIC) which was between the bridge and the Radar Room. All information came from the CIC to the Bridge and the Gun Director, who pointed the *Ward* in the right direction to shoot down incoming planes. Tension was thick enough in the CIC, as they say, to cut it.. Captain Brown plowed between the Bridge and CIC.

"Chief, what happens if the CIC takes a hit?"
"Each gun is own its own."

For the first time, I felt like I was really in a war zone. I was going into battle and I was scared. A shudder ran through me, which was noticed by the Chief.

"Easy, Mr. Rosenthal.
"Kamikazes?" I asked.
"What else?"

91

"How can they miss us? We're as long as a city block?"

"We run fast and shoot quickly."

"But how can you destroy them. They're as small as ants."

"Not ants. Bats."

"What's the difference?"

"Bats are bigger."

Our conversation was interrupted.

BRIDGE, RADAR. BEARING 235,
DISTANCE 15 MILES.
MANY BOGIES.
CLOSING.

The reporter in Rosenthal tried to maintain calm by writing down what was going on. *"Bearings. Estimated speed. Distance. The coordinates of life and death… And what the men were doing.*

"We're going to catch it," the Chief said.

In the Radar Room, tension had given way to confusion.

"The images… something's wrong," Kang said.

"Captain, something is happening here," Lansing repeated,

BRIDGE, RADAR. BEARING 235,
DISTANCE 7 MILES. MANY BOGIES.
STILL CLOSING.

Throughout the ship, lookouts peered into the afternoon haze. Nothing could be seen. Where were the bogies? They should be seen by now.

"Radar, what's going on?" the Captain demanded.

BRIDGE, RADAR, BEARING 235,
DISTANCE 5 MILES,
INCOMING.

"Where are they?"

"Easy Mr. Rosenthal. Easy."

"But we should be able to see them."

The sky was empty except for the blazing sun and a few scattered clouds. Then, as if by magic, the bogies appeared on the horizon flying toward the *Ward*. The lookouts shouted, "Many planes… Many planes …"

At that moment I wanted to hide. Bit where? The whole ship was a target.

"Hang in there, Mr. Rosenthal. Cover the story. You know, the *Ward's* crew under fire."

Suddenly, one of the lookouts screamed, "Not planes. Repeat, not planes. Birds. Hundreds of them."

A moment later hundreds of honking birds miraculously appeared, converging on the *Ward*, casting a shadow over the ship as they flew by. They were in an expanded V-formation, wing-tip to wing-tip, squadron, one squadron after another in an aerial display of precision and salvation. As they headed eastward, the sky was alive with the beating of their wings.

Around the ship, the response was immediate by men and officers alike.

"Geese," said Lansing.

"Lovely geese," replied Kang.

"Fucking geese," Boxer exclaimed.

"Shit," was Wallace's refrain.

"No plasma today," Doc Ferrell announced happily to Freeman.

"We're letting dinner get away," Willis yelled.

"Give us the recognition signal, you winged saviors," Marcus remarked quietly.

"Darn," said Schroeder. "Back home I could have knocked those guys out of the air."

"Hopefully, no double-header today," Warren pleaded. "And no extra innings, please."

"Granados summed it up for many, "Thank you, God.""

On the Bridge, the sentiment was universal.

Bert said, "Now that's a morale booster."

"Geese, not bats, our lucky day," Captain Brown acknowledged. Permit me to salute our flying friends." He added as he flipped a snappy salute skyward.

In the Log, Marcus wrote, "Geese, 1430. No weapons fired."

With my heart still pounding I promised himself that this story would not go untold. But who would believe it?

On the *195* a happy mood had replaced the sense of dread, which only a moment earlier had permeated the Bridge.

"I'll never hunt geese again," Verso confessed.
"Turkeys, yes, for Thanksgiving," Lopez yelled. "Not geese. Now I know why."
"Our luck held," Commander Atwood said simply.
"Ask them about the Rita movie again," Lopez piped. "We deserve it after bringing the *Ward* good luck."

"Captain, radar reports no other blips," Bert announced. "The screen is clear."

The Captain slumped in his chair. It seemed like a great weight had been removed from his shoulders. He looked around the Bridge at everyone before saying, "Secure from General Quarters."

He turned to Bert and said, "Pass the word to Point Bolo, Birds, not bats." He turned again at looked at Admiral Aaron Ward's sword in its display case on the Bridge, saying *"Maybe we won't need you today."*.

THE ENEMY

Part IV

TALL TALES

———————————⚬⚬⚬———————————

YOU MAY FIRE WHEN READY, GIDLEY.

COMMODORE GEORGE DEWEY

PRAISE THE LORD AND PASS THE AMMUNITION

LT. HOWELL MAURICE FORGY

THE NAVY IS BOTH A TRADITION AND A FUTURE --- AND
WE LOOK WITH PRIDE AND CONFIDENCE
IN BOTH DIRECTIONS.

ADMIRAL GEORGE ANDERSON

Chapter 15

COFFEE AND DONUTS

———————————————

<u>AFTERNOON WATCH – 1500 HOUR</u>

"Mr. Rosenthal, a hot mug of black coffee is what you need to sooth the nerves according to naval lore."

"Make it a big mug. I need a great deal of soothing."

The erstwhile reporter was talking to Thomas Blake, one of three cooks aboard the *Ward*. They were in the mess hall with many others, all still shaken by the "geese incident," as it was now called.

"I just learned I'm no hero."

"Join the club."

"Maybe I should just bury myself in my notebook, recording the flyover."

"Whatever helps. I sort of do that myself."

"You do?"

"I check the menu for the next meal. Always seems to work. Of course, geese are not one of our staples."

The cook said that with a chuckle, but the lesson wasn't lost on me.

At that moment the kitchen door opened and Elmer, the main cook, came into the room holding a large tray of newly baked donuts. Their aroma floated across the mess hall. Tough men swooned under their spell.

He was a small man, not much more than 5-foot in height with 45 years under his belt in this man's navy. A grainy three- day old beard pitted his face with stubble. He wore a white apron, which enfolded his body, covering his white shirt and pants. A large high white hat sat uneasily on his head. A cigarette dangled from the corner of his mouth. Inch-long ashes cling to the cigarette, seemingly about to fall if he took another step, or merely inhaled deeply. N one had ever seen Elmer without a cigarette in his mouth. And no one had ever seen ashes fall from his cigarettes. It was rumored that, even when he was sober, a perpetual three-day glow always seemed to mush his words. No one knew where he got the booze, or where he stashed it. Occasionally, an empty half-pint of Seagram 7 was discovered in the garbage about o be dumped overboard. The Captain, it was speculated, never pursued the issue. After all, Elmer was considered by many to be the best cook west of Pearl Harbor. Admirals wanted him on their ships, but he had a distinct dislike of *"brass."* He preferred being on a small ship with guys who enjoyed his donuts.

For some reason, Elmer placed the platter where I was seated.. There must have been a pyramid of thirty donuts all of them caked with a thick layer of chocolate.

"For the Navy's finest," he said with a twinkle in his eyes. "Anyone interested?"

A rush of men to the table answered his question. Arms extended, hands gyrated, and donuts were captured. Paul Costa, a machinist first class, spoke for all, saying, "What would we do without you, Elmer?"

"I'd cook a lot better if you'd fix the damn ventilators, Costa," Elmer quickly answered. "Hot as hell in the kitchen."

Then it happened, the unthinkable.

Before Costa could respond, the ash fell from Elmer's cigarette and curved into a flight path, which would carry it to the pile of donuts.

Everyone was astounded. This had never happened before. Maybe the kitchen was even hotter than hell and poor Elmer was finally running out of gas.

Everyman in the room watched the ashes slow descent into the baked delights, sort of like a suicide plane descending on the *Ward*. Acting quickly out of some gastronomic survival instinct, Costa grabbed a *Life Magazine*, and moved it back and forth over the doughnuts to fan away the ashes.

"O.K., Elmer, Costa said. I get the picture. I'll fix the ventilators first as soon as the damage control pumps are checked."

The platter draw the men to it like a bear to honey. Most of the men took two chocolate donuts. I took one. My stomach craved three, but I didn't want to start a riot.

"Costa," Elmer bellowed, "You'd fix the damn ventilators if they had handlebars and a siren on them. Damn motorcycle cop."

"You have no call to speak like that, Elmer. I liked being a cop. I loved my motorcycle. The siren was great. Click it on and hit the gas. The road opens up for you. You were the man flying down the highway of life at 80 miles an hour. People respected you, or at least, they were afraid of you, and they sure as hell got out of your way. As for the young women… They fell in love with you. Must have been the leather pants and jacket, or maybe the sun glasses"

"What do you think, Mr. Reporter? Elmer asked. "Was it Costa's leather or his dimples that attracted the ladies?"

I was unprepared for Elmer's question. And why call me, *"Mr. Reporter?"* I just wanted to be Rosenthal.

Elmer had a shady grin on his face. Costa just glared.

101

"I would suggest his shiny badge."

"Excellent answer," Costa said with obvious delight. "Here, have the last chocolate donut."

I accepted his offer and enjoyed a big bite. I had to. Costa might still have his badge.

"Wise answer," said Elmer. "Don't forget to give my donuts the coverage they deserve, and there's no need to talk about the ashes. Right?"
"Right."

Elmer reached for the now empty platter and at that very moment my life got further complicated. Boxer Jernigan entered the Mess Hall, proclaiming, *"Donut time."* He looked at empty platter and my lips encrusted with chocolate, and grew red faced.

"You bastards ate all the chocolate donuts."
"The Lord provided, proclaimed Granados."
"Now listen, Padre…"

Finishing his donut with obvious relish and teasing for Boxer for all he was worth, Chief Marcus spoke to Boxer.
"Yummy."

Holding a partially eaten donut Warren announced, *"My favorite."*

"I'll cut your bloody heart out."
"Now, why would you do that?" asked Granados. "You know Elmer is going to make more. Isn't that right, Elmer?"
"Right. So cool off, Boxer.. There'll be another batch in about, oh, let's say, five minutes. I make a special plate just for you."
"You bums didn't even leave one for me," Boxer said in a scolding voice. "You stole my share."
"Stole? Hardly." said Kang. " We picked carefully in your absence."
"That's bull shit!"
"That about covers it," someone interjected.

Boxer turned to me. "Do you think this is fair?"

"It will be fair if Elmer adds a lot more chocolate to the very special doughnut plate he's going to prepare solely for you. This is to make up for any indiscretion."

Boxer walked over to me. His face was rock hard. Not a hint as to how he felt about my response. I was prepared for the worst, wondering if my burial at sea would be heartfelt by all.

Boxer put one large, powerful arm around my neck, and then blossomed with a huge smile.

"I like this, kid."

The excitement over, Elmer reentered the conversation by announcing the evening menu.

"Listen up my hearties, for lunch the menu will be your favorites --- beans, more beans, and even more beans teamed with hot dogs, mashed potatoes, peas, biscuits, milk, cake, and leafy salad for the pussies in this group."

A collective groan curled up from the assembled men. *"Ugh."* Then a voice barked out.

"Coffee! Where's the hot coffee?" Boxer asked. "Hot coffee now, Elmer."

Now if bunker fuel is what fueled the *Ward*, or gunpowder was necessary to fire an explosive out of the five-inch guns, than coffee is what puts the *"go"* in the Navy. Coffee, hot and fragrant, puts starch in a guys back when the bogie are flying around. Coffee, always brewing, always perking, permits a guy to focus on his job. It was an unwritten law on the *Ward*; good coffee protected the ship, good coffee brought good luck.

"I'll be right back with a pot," Elmer said as left in haste.

The door to the mess hall opened again and this time Bert came into the room escorted by another chief, Chuck McLennan, who was in charge of the munitions crews. Bert announced, "I'll never talk ill of a goose again."

There was a collective nod and a general sigh. Everyone realized how lucky the ship had been. No suicide planes and the talk about donuts and motorcycles, ventilators, and coffee exercised the demons feasting upon the crew.

The verbal jousting ended with McLennan saying to no one in particular, Take good care of Mr. Rosenthal. He needs a lunch and lots of stories for the folks back home. "Laverne, why don't you tell Mr. Rosenthal about Marpi Point."

"I can't. Get someone else."
"Doc Ferrell?"
"No."
"Costa?"
"Skip me."

The Mess Room grew somber. No one was talking, not a word.

"Perhaps later," McLennan said quietly.

ELMER'S STORY

Elmer had always been a cook. Cooked in roadside cafes, diners, coffee houses, and a few upscale restaurants. He had also cooked for the Army during the First World War, then in the C.C.C. during the Depression, and in '40-41, for the U.S. Forestry Service. Now he was in another war.

He reminded me that it doesn't matter where you are, the customer always wants the same thing, lots of food, hot, and at a cheap price. It doesn't matter how hard you work either because gripers and foul-mouthed people are everywhere.

Elmer had never been married. He liked his women few and far between and not on a permanent basis.

Some said that he drank on the job. In truth that was probably an accurate statement. He explained to me that brandy or a pint of bourbon was a Navy tradition and never hurt a cook.

He smoked before the war and would continue after the war. And, yes it's true, occasionally a few ashes fell into the main dish, but no one ever died from a few ashes. Perhaps from his cooking, but not the ashes.

Every cook, he suggested, has a few favorite concoctions, secrets of the trade, and a few favorite customers. He took pride in dressing up the beans. They were still beans but the sauce can make all the difference, and Elmer knew sources. As to his favorite customer, at least for this week, he had one.

As he told me, "I'm going to bake a big, beautiful birthday cake for Laverne. He'll be 18 in a few days and we're going to celebrate right --- chocolate frosting for the boy and "rubbers" from the crew to make his next leave memorable. Naturally, his folks will hear about the cake, but that's it. I'm sure looking forward to his birthday."

Elmer's philosophy of life was mess hall simple. "Sure it was true, we've got guns above deck, and engines below deck. We've got officers over there and able-bodied seaman here, but what connects all of them is the mess hall where good food, good conversation, and good morale all come together. And that is where I come in. I'm the cook."

Chapter 16

MARPI POINT

AFTERNOON WATCH - 1530 HOURS

I listened as Jernigan held sway in the mess hall, which was now very quiet, if not subdued. Donut and coffee smiles were gone. A strange sadness pervaded the room.

I had urged him to do so. A reporter's curiosity pushed me to know what happened and why the men were so taciturn about the topic.

"It was early last year," Boxer said, "when the whole thing started. The *Ward* was part of the invasion of Saipan, another Japanese infested island, but not a little one. Saipan was in the Mariana Islands, about 1,500 miles from Japan in the Central Pacific. It was big island crawling with the 30,000 of the Emperor's troops.

"The Marines landed on June 15, 1944, and 20,000 of them made it to shore by evening," Al Warren added. Almost 3,100 of them would never leave the island."

"It was even worse for the Japanese. Over 29,000 lost their lives," Norm Willis added bitterly. They wouldn't surrender."

"The big chiefs said we needed the island for the new B-29's rolling out of Boeing factories," Jose Granados added. "We needed an airbase from which to bomb Japan."

"That place changed my life," Laverne said in a low voice.

"It changed all of us, " Little Bear added. "It changed us forever."

Why was this island invasion different than the others? Why were these tough guys speaking with cracks in the voices and moist eyes? It couldn't be just the American deaths? Those were to be expected, though no one wanted to volunteer to make a prediction come true. No, something else was involved. I wanted to know what.

Boxer continued, saying, "The Nips wouldn't surrender. Just like on Iwo. They would commit suicide before dishonoring themselves. They cut open their bellies with ancestral swords. They exploded grenades against their chests."

"They charged into the Marine lines at the end with nothing more than bayonets attached to bamboo sticks," Wallace pointed out with a shrug. "Can you imagine that?"

"Some just threw rocks at the Marines," said a sad voice. "Rocks! They were out of bullets."

"It seemed like they wanted the Marines to kill them," remarked Doc Ferrell.

"But that wasn't the worst of it," Marcus said.

What could possibly be worse, I wondered. I was about to find out.

"We were less than 100 yards from the shore when it started," Boxer said. "We were giving the Marines close in support. We could see everything."

At that moment the men realized that Captain Brown was in the room listening to the conversation. Everyone jumped to attention, but the Captain stopped this with a quiet, "As ease, sailors. Please continue, Mr. Jernigan."

The Captain sat down and Elmer poured him a cup of coffee. I don't think I've ever seen a face as despondent as Captains Brown was at that moment.

Boxer continued, "We were off Marpi Point, a rocky area with cliff towering more than a hundred feet above us. We began to see people gathering at the point," he said with a faltering voice.

Lansing helped him. "The Japanese commanders convinced the Chamorros, the original inhabitants of the island, that the Americans would kill them, but only after torturing them and raping the woman. They convince the Korean slave laborers and civilians from Okinawa that this was their fate too if the Americans captured them."

I noticed the men were looking down at their shoes, anywhere but at each other. No one wanted to make eye contact.

"Panicked civilians were herded to the cliffs and told to jump off the cliffs and into the course sea below, or onto a rock strewn beach that patiently awaited their falling bodies," Captain Brown said. "Many mothers threw their babies and children over the cliffs before jumping themselves."

"If you didn't jump," Lansing pointed out, "you were shot."

The Captain stood, glanced around the room before looking up, as if pleading to God, as if making a death confession on a cold bed.

"I tried to get them to stop. I brought the *Ward* in even closer. We could almost spit on the island. We were only 50 yards off the beaches."

Hundreds of civilians are seen, men, women, and children on top of the cliff. Japanese soldiers are all around them, yelling at them, pricking them with swords and bayonets, even firing their weapons at the people. Then the crowd begins to jump, a few at first, then more, and finally a torrent --- much like buffalo driven by Indians and yapping dogs over cliffs in Colorado. Soon the sea was full of bodies

MARPI POINT AFTER THE BATTLE

"The Captain put me on the loud speaker," Kang added. "I pleaded with the people in Japanese. I tried to get them to stop. They wouldn't listen. There was this one woman ..."

"I remember.' Laverne said. "It was terrible."

A woman emerged in full view and stumbled across the cliff plateau to the edge. In her arms she held a child. She stood swaying back and forth, staring down at the jagged rocks protruding menacingly from the surf below. Suddenly, the woman, still clutching the child, and, paying no heed to Kang leaped from the cliff and fell to the water below. She seemed to fall in slow motion. There was an audible thump. That awful sound was caused by her striking other human beings and not the rocks.

"Worst moment of this damn war," Captain Brown said.

I was told later that the men knew Captain Brown, though it was never said aloud, was not the same again after that. He was quieter. He seemed immensely sad. He was withdrawn for short periods. He seemed to age before their eyes. Oh, he still demanded drills and reports, duties and tasks completed on time. He continued to instill discipline and courage, but he was different. A bit of his soul was lost that day at Marpi Point.

A bit of all their souls was lost that day, I thought.

"Got the story, Mr. Rosenthal?" Jernigan asked.
"What kind of war is this?" I heard myself asking. "What kind of war?"

MARCUS' STORY

He was the guy in charge of records, the office keeper of the Ward. Nothing happened in writing, which didn't pass through his hands short of personal letters and diaries.

He had been in the Great War --- World War I. Turning 18 in 1915, he joined the Navy to see the world, or at least to get out of Philadelphia. He logged four years in the Navy, mainly in the North Atlantic aboard destroyers, the old four pipers. After the war, he remained in the Reserves. That's where Uncle Sam found him after Pearl Harbor.

He spent considerable time on the U.S.S. Saufley before being transferred to the Ward. The Saufley was a good ship. It saw lots of action in the early part of the war when things were really dicey, Guadalcanal in particular. He picked up a Purple Hart in '43.

Marcus was actually older than the Captain. Often the new recruits confused him with Captain Brown. He had the age and gray hair, but not the position, or a raise in pay. Still, he enjoyed the temporary honor.

He was Jewish. He tried to keep quite about his religious background, but the word always got out. Some of the guys called him a Jew-boy, not really a nice term, especially for an older guy. On rare occasions when they had too much to drink, he was called worse. There was nothing he could do about it.

Marcus wanted to be in the Atlantic theater. With the Japanese, it was war. With the Germans, it was personal. The Navy had other ideas and routed

111

him to the Pacific. His son, Martin, who was in the Army Air force, had the same fate. Though each was in the Pacific, it took six months for a letter to pass between them.

Before the war, he worked for the Post Office in San Francisco. It was a good job during the Depression, especially after spending two years in the C.C.C. Postal pay was modest but it was steady. You could bank on it. Anyway, it beat being out of work. Most probably, he'd go back to the Post Office when the war is over.

But that was for later. Aboard the Ward, he had only one concern. He wanted to see his son again, who was out there somewhere in the Pacific with suicide planes looking for both of them.

Chapter 17

THE SQUALL

The mess hall vacated. Relating the Marpi Point story had left a bad taste in everyone's mouth. Not even Elmer's chocolate donuts and stiff black coffee would remove the stench.

I found myself alone in the mess hall with my notes. What would I write someday? How would I explain this horror? At the moment, I had no answer, only the conviction that the story would be told.

As I considered these questions, far to the west on Japan's southernmost island, the "bats" were preparing for their flight to Okinawa, May 3, 1945. Only after the war did I learn what took place and why?

FLASHBACK – THE PILOTS

Japanese war films showed young men drinking rice wine in a large airdrome. Some are praying before a sacred shrine. Others are donning a "hachimaki," a bandana-like cloth worn tied around the forehead. Some of the white clothes had calligraphy on them. A few had a red sun symbol.

Outside of the building on the airstrip were various aircraft being readied for the attack --- Bettys, Zekes, and Vals --- medium bombers, fighter planes, and dive bombers. The planes are mostly old --- what was left of Japan's air power. Each plane carried only enough fuel to reach the American fleet.

The pilots were young, high school and college age. Adhering to their Samurai warrior past, the white cloths tied around their heads signified their willingness to die for the Emperor. In death there was hope. In death, there was glory.

At the time, we considered the Japanese pilots fanatics. The truth was far different.

They belonged to the *toubetsu kogeki tai* --- which literally means a *" special attack unit."* The word *shinpu*, which meant divine wind or kamikaze, provided a fuller more accurate rendering --- "divine wind special attack unit."

THE ATTACK

The term kamikaze is derived from two words --- *kami* is the word for god, spirit, or divinity. *Kaze* referred to the wind. As one word, they referred to the divine wind. The word originated in 1274 and 1281 to describe the great storms, which battered and dispersed the Mongolian invasion fleets bearing down upon Japan. For the Japanese, the Mongolians had returned with flags ablaze with stars and stripes. If nature had not yet provided another typhoon to destroy the barbarians, the young pilots would.

Based on the traditions in Samurai life and the Bushido code, the unit placed emphasis on loyalty and honor unto death. The goal of crippling American warships was understood as a last attempt to save the empire in a manner similar to *"banzai charges."*

FLASHBACK – INSTRUCTIONS

The pilots were listening to last minute directions from their flight officer. He held a model plane and was showing his pilots, one last time, how to dive on the American ships, especially the carriers. With defeat everywhere, with the B-29's raining daily death upon Japanese cities, with her navy scattered and sunk, with her armies fighting from caves on Okinawa, the Japanese sun was setting. Only one last desperate measure was possible; fling young men into the air on a one way trip against the American fleet, one last effort to stop the defeat of Japan --- suicide for glory. The kamikaze pilots were prepared to die for "Shikishima," a poetic name for Japan.

Contrary to most American propaganda, the young Japanese pilots did not lust for the opportunity to kill themselves. What motivated them was the desperate situation of Japan. Those who died at the Alamo would understand.

FLASHBACK – THE PLANES

Mechanics prepared the planes for battle. Fuel lines extended to the plane, enough fuel to reach the American fleet, not enough fuel to return to the base. Bomb racks were adjusted for their angry cargo --- one large lethal bomb to destroy a warship. The engine hoods were closed. The pilots walked toward their planes to inspect them. The plane's normal role was converted to that of a manned missile.

PREPARING ZEROS FOR AN ATTACK

My thoughts were interrupted. Lansing and Kang. They rejoined me for a cup of coffee a few minutes before the *First Dog Watch* --- 1600 hours.

"Well, Mr. Reporter, we thought we'd cheer you up with a few raindrops," Lansing said in a causal manner. "You do need cheering up, don't you?"

There it was again. I was no longer Robert Rosenthal. I was Mr. Reporter Rosenthal. My first name had been high jacked.

"Raindrops sounds better than Marpi Point."
"Especially when they are gifts from the gods," added Kang.
"I don't understand."
"You will," Lansing said.

Lansing paused to add considerable sugar and cream to his coffee making it a kind of mini-milk shake. He caught my eye watching him.

"I need the boost. This evening could be a long one."
"He gets a funny feeling now and then," Kang suggested.
"Has he ever been right?" I asked.
"Never, but he only has to be right once."
"Let's hope your failure record remains unblemished," I retorted.
"Amen," Lansing said. "Now, as to the raindrops..."

Lansing and Kanag were in the Radar Room five days ago almost to the minute. It began with Lansing's uneasiness. He was looking at the radar copes.

"Something bothering you, Sir? The screen is clear. All the screens are clear."

"You know, I trust the radar to show me what it sees… problem is, it doesn't see everything, does it?"

"Something out there?"

"There's always something out there."

"Yeah."

A sailor interrupted them. He informed them that they were tracking a squall spotted earlier. It had gotten bigger and closer, about a mile off to the north, apparently with heavy rainfall.

Lansing responded, saying he would pass the word to the Captain. "Keep an eye on it. Funny, the way it just appeared out of nowhere."

"The squall kept moving closer to our heading, and the closer it got, the bigger it looked," Kang explained. A light rain began to fall on the *Ward* and beyond this misty curtain we could see a torrent a water flooding the sea.

FLASHBACK – THE SQUALL

The squall was a towering water geyser, a wall of water flowing from some unlocked celestial faucet. It whirls toward the Ward, then backs off before moving again in the ship's direction. The air was heavy with mist. The sun seemed to be drifting away, shielded and obscured by this primeval force.

Kang piped in, "We all wanted the Captain to steer away from it, but he refused to stand clear. He stayed near it playing a cat-and-mouse game, always just staying out of range."

"The men on the bridge thought he was crazy, "Lansing said with a smile. "But he was crazy like a fox."

"He would circle near the squall, neither running from it, nor turning into it," Kang said. "We were like two magnets attacked to each other by physical laws, yet dancing with each other at a distance."

"Then it happened," Lansing said with glee, "and the Captain was proven right in his actions."

"Then what happened?" I said.

"It was the craziest thing," Lansing offered.

"What…?" I blurted out.

"They came out of nowhere," Kang shared.

"Who came…?"

"Two Jap dive bombers."

"They had been hiding in the cloud cover above the squall," Kang noted.

"Dive bombers! The radar never picked them up."

"The squall masked their presence, but somehow the Captain knew," Lansing said with pride."

"Mental radar?" I asked.

"Maybe."

"You guys are keeping me in suspense. What happened?"

FLASHBACK – INSIDE THE MAELSTROM

The Ward, turned into the squall, even as the planes sighted and dove on her. For a moment she leaned hard over her keel giving the impression she was no longer a man-of-war, but rather a sleek sailing ship with wind in her canvas. Entering the squall, the Ward was immediately enveloped in a blessed shower, which poured over every inch of her in a continuous torrent.

Inside the squall, the Captain danced with Father Neptune. Where the squall went, the Ward followed, bobbing and weaving within the safety in this drenching.

Outside the squall, the two planes circled the squall unable to see the Ward hidden by the saving spray.

"What a story! " I cried. "Unbelievable."

"What a shower," Lansing said with zeal. "The squall pounded us so hard the Japs couldn't see us."

"We spent thirty minutes in that bath tub moving with it in very direction," Kang said. "If it went north, we went north. If it went west, we went west. If it stopped, we stopped."

"The boys in the engine room earned their pay that day," Lansing added.

"The pilots couldn't out wait you?" I asked.

"Fuel," said Lansing. "We had plenty. They didn't. They had to blink first. They had to find another mouse. The cat left."

"Well, Mr. Writer, asked Kang, "you will write about this?"

"Already know the chapter title."

"Which is?" Lansing asked.

"Something Out There."

ARBRAHAM FREEMAN'S STORY

Let's start with his history and name. Abraham Freeman was the fourth Abraham in his family dating back to the Civil War. His great-great grandfather was born in 1866 shortly after Bobby Lee surrendered to U.S. Grant. His mother worshipped the President who had signed the Emancipation Proclamation freeing the slaves. Abraham was her choice to remember the stricken President, who had brought them out of economic bondage. Her husband took Freeman as their last name, a logical choice since they were freed men at last.

If Abraham survived this war, there would be another Abraham. The Freeman family would continue.

His folks had been tenant farmers in Alabama near Montgomery since 1865. Before that, they worked the same land as slaves. Tenant farming was hard. Abraham's family worked hard all year on borrowed funds from the landlord. They harvested a meager crop and were lucky if they came out with a small profit. It wasn't slavery, but it was economic bondage.

Abraham was working on the farm when the war started. He decided he needed to get into it. The Navy picked him up and landed him on the Ward.

Sometimes he felt like a tenant sailor in the Navy. Though he applied for other positions in the training school, he was placed in the food preparation service. In other words, he worked in the kitchen. In time, he discovered the Navy's dirty little secret. Negroes tended to be placed in the kitchen. Whites worked the guns, ran the engines, and served in the radar room. Negroes fought the war with pots and pans. It was a form of unofficial l Jim Crowism.

Abraham had one overriding desire. He wanted to prove he could fight. He wanted to prove his worth with the guns. He wanted to do this before the war was over.

After the war, he planned to go to school. He wanted to get off the farm. If possible, he would take advantage of the new G.I. Bill he had heard about. He wanted to attend a college. His high school teacher said he was smart. He wanted to prove her right. All he had to do was survive the war, and afterwards, his buddy Wallace.

Chapter 18

THE CRAPPER

I sat in the mess hall staring at my notebook. Though I had been on the *Ward* less than eight hours, the lined pages were already brimming with my personal notations scrolled chicken-like in my haste to get everything down. Naturally, I would never admit to questionable cursive writing or a penchant for misspelling words. Rather, I liked to think the Navy had its secret code and I had mine.

I was about to stroll around the ship when a crowd burst in upon me: Chief McLennan, Boxer Jernigan, Laverne, Willis, Lansing, and Rossi. It was like a convention of my new friends.

"Still here," Mr. Reporter?" the Chief asked.
"Just leaving."
"Stick around for some coffee, kid," said Boxer almost as a demand.
"Okay, buy my name is Robert."
"Make it shorter," said Lansing. "How about Rob?"
"Sounds good to me," Rossi chimed in with zest.
"It has a nice ring to it," remarked Willis.

Nicknames… I'm convinced it's a guy thing, and in the Navy it's an addiction. Looking around I realized I was now the beneficiary of three possibilities. Mr. Reporter just didn't do it for me. Rosenthal was okay, as was Robert. Rob actually had a nice ring to it. Jimmy Cagney would like it. *Byline by Rob*… Nice. *Rob's Corner*…Good title for my hopeful future column in a daily paper somewhere. *Rob's Report*… Now that was nice!

"Guys, a deal. OK?"
"We're going to play cards?" Laverne asked.
"No. We're going to settle on my name."
"You already have a name," Boxer replied.
"True, Boxer, at least three new ones since I boarded the *Ward*."
"So what?" He asked
"I'd like to be called just one."
"Okay," said the Chief, "which one?"
"Rob."
"Excellent choice, kid," said Lansing. "It shows you have good taste."
"Not kid, Rob!"
"As you say pencil pusher," Willis said with a big smile.

There was no way out of this. The gods had tagged me with an excess of names. I would have to live with it until Rob stuck. Robert Rosenthal was becoming a figment of my imagination.

"You guys win. But I do have one question I hope you will grant."
"Yeah!" Boxer said. "What is it?"
"How did you get a name like Boxer, Boxer?"

The convention concerning *"nicknames"* suddenly ended and the room went deadly quiet. Later, I would learn that no one asked Boxer that question and lived. The Chief broke the silence. "Oh, go ahead Boxer. Tell this poor chap how you got your name. He's not worth throwing overboard. Anyway, he can't write on wet paper while swallowing salt water."

Poor chap --- another tag for my lengthening list. Looking at Boxer's reddening face and bulging muscles, I began to think this newest name was quite appropriate. If Boxer came at me, I would be a poor chap. But that didn't happen. Boxer sat back and slowly calmed himself. I'll never know why.

"You guys all know the story," he said. "I'll bore you."
"Rob doesn't," said Lansing. "And he won't be bored. Trust me."
"Come on, Boxer. I love this story," Laverne said quietly.
"It will make my day," Willis added.

Boxer was resistant. "No way." He held up a plain donut and stared hard at the group. "Not After what you guys did!"

"Where you get that musty old thing?" the Chief asked.
"My business."
"I'd like to hear the story, " I said cautiously.

Boxer didn't say anything, not a word. We were at an impasse. Then, mysteriously, magically, Chief Marcus produced an uneaten chocolate donut, which he offered to Boxer, and which was taken without a word. Three quick bites and the donut disappeared.

"Boxer, come on. Tell Rob about the *Panay*."
"What's a *Panay*? " Laverne asked half-heartedly.

With that Boxer nearly exploded.. "Each time I do this you ask the same dumb question. What the hell do they teach you kids today?"
"I never finished high school," Danny shared with a big sigh.
"If it's good, I'll file your story first --- 'The Boxer at RPS 10.' How does that sound, Boxer?" I asked.

Boxer looked around the room. He realized that he is holding court. His gaze finally rested on Laverne, sympathetically.

"Never finished high school myself, kid. O.K., I'll tell the story. It was back in'37..."

FLASHBACK – THE U.S.S. PANAY

The U.S.S. Panay is seen on the Yangtze River in China. The month was December; the day was the 12th. The ship was a small American gunboat, twin-stacked, trim in white and buff paint. Two very large American flags were painted on the ship's awnings. A large cotton flag hung from the mast. In China the flags identified the ship as American and therefore neutral in the Sino-Japanese conflict. The ship was moored near Nanking to rescue American citizens before the Japanese captured the city.

"I was in the pre-war Navy, the Asiatic fleet. We were near Nanking to get American nationals out before the Japanese bombed the city. The Captain was a good man, James Joseph Hughes. We were a good crew. We all thought the flags would keep us safe. We were wrong."

FLASHBACK – THE ATTACK

Six Japanese planes attacked the Panay. Bombs were falling. The ship was strafed and almost immediately fire and explosions occurred.. The ship began to list heavily to port.

"Our pumps couldn't control the flooding. We started to sink. Pearl Harbor came earlier for us."

"I like the next part better," said Laverne with obvious enthusiasm.

While Boxer had been talking, Elmer reentered the room with another platter of donuts, which he placed before the big guy with a flourish.

"What do you think, Boxer? Is this a worthy bribe? Tell them what else happened." With a shit-for-eating smile, Elmer remarked, "It's not everyday that a man gets caught with his pants off."

Eyeing the doughnuts, Boxer continued his story after first enclosing his large arms around the plate.

"Listen, you clowns, when you have to take a shit, you don't contact Tokyo for permission. Christ, how'd I know they would attack while I was on the crapper?"

As if he was hearing the story for the first time, Laverne said, "On the crapper! No way."

Willis chirped, "Son-of-a-bitch!".

"How appropriate," Marcus said with a hearty laugh.

"What'd you do?" I asked in all innocence.

"I took the fastest crap in history and jumped into the Yangtze. What the hell do you think I did?"

"The ship sank, didn't it, Boxer?".

"Never had a chance, Rob."

"And Roosevelt didn't do much," I added.

"You know your history."

"He sent a stiff letter to Tokyo. Threatened to cut off scrap iron and crude oil exports."

"I'm impressed," Boxer said. "You do know your history."

"The Japanese government apologized. They called the attack an accident ... a mistake. Even provided some money for the *"incident,"* as they called it. They thought the *Panay* was a Chinese gunboat."

Boxer coughed up a bitter laugh. "There was no mistake. Not with those giant American flags painted on the awning and our big flag flowing in the wind. Mistake, my ass! Those bastards knew exactly what they were doing."

"And your name, Boxer?" Danny asked.

"Trying getting caught with your boxer shorts off ... See what they call you!"

The men all laughed. No question, it was a good story.

WALLACE'S STORY

He was the 'redneck aboard the ship. You know, the guy from the deep South chewing brownish tobacco and spitting out prejudice, a poorly education man who was raised by disciples of Jim Crow laws. He's the guy who didn't want to swim with Negroes in public pools, or drink from the same water fountains. He wanted to sit in the front of the bus, and avoid eating in the same restaurant room. As to living in the same area or attending school with former slaves that would never happen. He referred to himself as a paid up member of the KKK in good standing.

To quote him directly, "I'm a redneck, and like other Americans, I demand my right to be bigoted."

Though limited in his education, Wallace was not dumb, and from his point-of-view, his views made sense. I remember him telling me...

"I know some... you know, the educated from the North, who think they're so smart... they think I'm crude, even repulsive in my views. But, hell, take a look at them. They talk a good story --- 'lets be nice to the Negroes.' Well, check out where they live, and where their kids go to school... Not a nice picture, is it? At least in the South, we don't fool ourselves --- not like the Yankees."

He admitted to me that life on the Ward could be tough for him. He didn't mean the fighting. Heck, he had been fighting someone all his life. The Nips were just another Negro of a different color to be smacked down and put into their place.

He realized he was pig-headed, but that's the way he was brought up. That's the way he lived his life. And, as he liked to say, before you bitch, just remember I'm not telling you how to live your life, so don't tell me how to live mine.

When reminded there would be changes after the war, he was adamant in his views. Segregation wouldn't end. With pride, he pointed out that his family didn't fight at Cold Harbor, Vicksburg, and Richmond to give Negroes the vote and equality. No sir, they fought to maintain States Rights --- to keep the federal government off their backs, to leave them alone. Now if the states want to end segregation on their own, okay, that's fine with me. I'll still live where I want to.

His comments about Freeman were instructive. "I'll admit," he said, "he's good sailors. He does his job. O.K. I just don't want to live next door to him.. Do you?"

He liked his job in Mount 51. He really liked the idea of shooting down those "fucking little Jap bastards."

Chapter 19

CROSSING THE EQUATOR

FIRST DOG WATCH – 1500 HOURS

The convention ended. Except for Marcus everyone headed back to his duty station in a rush. We, however, sauntered toward his office, where I wanted to use the *Ward's* one typewriter. Inside the crowded room, I noticed a photograph of the Yeoman taped to the metal desk. Marcus was in his Navy shorts dripping wet on the deck of some ship. Pointing to it, I asked, "What's this?"

"Initiation."
"To what? For what?"
"Crossing the line for the first time."
"Which line?"
"The Equator."
"Sounds interesting. Care to share with the uninitiated?"
"Sure."

Marcus untapped the picture, glanced at it for a moment, and then explained to me why I might avoid the Equator in the future.

"I was on the *U.S.S. Saufley* earlier in the war. She was a nice ship, the *465*, named after Richrd C. Saufley, who was killed flying an early experimental Navy plane. We crossed the Equator on the way to Australia, then Guadalcanal. The ship had an initiation for men crossing that line of latitude for the first time."

Guadalcanal… For the Navy and the Marines, this had been their *Valley Forge* in 1942-43, when the Japanese had headed southward toward Australia. In a terrible six-month struggle, the Marines prevailed on land, while the Navy fought the Japanese to a tie offshore; 26-capital ships were lost by each side, many of which sank in the Iron Bottom Sound. This was the first time the Naval forces of the Emperor had been stopped.

"Was it your first time? I asked.
"No. I crossed during the Great War."
"What happened?"

"First I had to crawl through a tunnel of garbage the crew had collected for days. What a mess. Then I had to do it again through a cloth target used for gunnery practice. Inside it was all slimy and wet. If I stopped crawling, someone would whack me on my tail. That kept me going, let me tell you. Those whacks hurt."
"Sounds awful."
"Not as bad as the "pollywog trial.""
"The what?"
"Pollywogs…first timers across the Equator."
"And the trial?"

Marcus thought about that for a moment before answering in his dry, matter-of-fact manner.

"The day before the trial, all pollywogs were left alone. We were free to move about the ship. The older guys even covered our work stations. We had a great time just goofing off. But while we were enjoying ourselves, the experienced guys were going through our bunks and lockers. They were gathering evidence to be used against us in a mock trail. At the trial there was a king and queen, and their baby. They were the fattest guys on the ship. The king had on a diaper and we had to get on our knees and kiss his belly. If you flinched while doing this, you would get hit with an electric rod or be smacked by someone. The trial ended with our hair being cut and then being dumped into a canvas bagful of water."

Marcus stopped to catch his breath. The Navy and its rituals... Thank god, Okinawa was north of the Equator.

"I guess you never wanted to do that to another guy."

"Are you kidding? I can't wait until it's my turn to do the smacking."

"Another story?"

"Right. The *Saufley* had a new group of sailors and we were headed for the line. We were prepared to give the pollywogs hell. We were with another ship, the *USS Little*, and that was the problem."

"Why?"

"They had a dead sailor abroad. He needed to be buried at sea. There are no Equator celebrations when there's a burial. Those pollywogs got lucky that day, but not that poor fellow in the weighted canvas."

"I expect you would show me no mercy if we cross the line."

"None."

"Well then, I better type a few minutes and then I'm off to see Chief Rossi to learn about the *Ward's* history."

"Bring a thick notepad. There were three *Wards*."

Chapter 20

HISTORY LESSONS

———————————◦———————————

<u>FIRST DOG WATCH – 1700 HOURS</u>

Marcus accompanied me to the bridge, where now familiar faces were hard at work --- Captain Brown, Bert, and Chief Rossi. The Captain turned to me and with a shy grin said, "Rob… That's the nickname they hung on you, right?"

The Captain always seemed to know things before anyone else.

"Rob it is, sir."
"Well, it could have been worse."
"I guess I owe a debt to Lansing."
"We all owe a debt. Check this out."

The Captain directed my attention to the old sword encased in its place of honor, a hollowed relic of a bygone age.

"Old Admiral Ward used this against the Spanish in '98, 1898, directing his big guns by sweeping motions of this sword. Of course, he never had to worry about death defying kamikazes."
"From what I heard, he probably would do the same thing today."

"Could be."

The sword, circa 1890, reflected the late afternoon sun. It had a mystical quality to it. One had the feeling that, if swords could speak, it would have much to say.

"Manila Harbor! Broadsides! Swords! I'm afraid I missed my time."
"Or he missed our time, Captain," I added.
"There's that."
"Sunset of Spain's empire," Bert reminded us.
"And now Japan's," I remarked philosophically.
"Not a moment too soon," Chief Rossi argued.

The Captain turned from the sword, peered off to the western horizon before asking, "Sunset is at 1900?"

No one was fooled. The Captain knew exactly when sunset would occur.

"Yes, sir," Bert answered.
"We can expect our friends within the next two hours, Bert."
"Yes, sir."
"Witching time, Rob," the Captain said, "when the bats come out of the western sun-filled sky."

"Sir, should we go to general quarters at 1830 as scheduled? Bert asked.
"Make it 1730."
"That early?"

The men look at the Captain. They have been with him long enough to accept and trust his instincts. Still, they were a bit startled by his decision to go to battle stations so early. The chain of command ruled. It would be "business as usual" at RPS 10, only a little sooner this late afternoon.

"Pass the message to the *Little e* and the others, Bert."
"Right."
"Chief, have you shown Rob the photographs?"

"No, sir."

"Well, get at it. It's time he learned about the *Ward's* history."

"As you say…"

Rossi grabbed my arm in a friendly grip, saying, "Time to go to school."

He walked me back to the mess hall, where he said, "Look at this wall. You've passed it a few times already, but I'm sure you didn't take time to really see it. Well, look at it now."

I gazed at the wall. Pinned to it on a large corkboard were many photographs, each neatly identified by pinned cards.

"The Captain lets me enjoy my avocation by maintaining the board and sharing the ship's history with the crew. He thinks it's a good for morale. What do you think?"

"Sure, especially if the history is fascinating."

"That it is, since we're talking about three *Wards*. Let's start here."

He pointed to a picture of an older Admiral Aaron Ward, very dignified and strong in character. "It all started here in 1898. He led the *USS Wasp* against the pride of the Spanish fleet, the *Don Jorge Juan*. In a quick scrap, he defeated the larger ship/"

"Quite a guy."

"The Navy thought so. He was promoted to Command and lived until 1919. Then the Navy decided to name a ship after him. He deserved it. He had spent 42-years in the service."

"The first *Ward*?" I asked.

"A new destroyer from the Bath Iron Works in Maine--- the *DD132*." That was back in1919."

"DD?"

"What you're standing on, a *"Tin Can,"* a *"Can Do"* ship --- a destroyer. There are over 200 of them in this invasion fleet. Here, check out this photo."

U.S.S. AARON WARD (DD 132)

The photo showed the first *Ward*. She was beautiful, gleaming in the sun, a new flush-deck destroyer with four stacks."

"Guess who christened the ship? Right, the admiral's daughter did the job. How about that?"

"What happened to the *DD132*?"

"That's a good question, which, I'm afraid I can't answer. She served in the Great War and between wars until Roosevelt gave her away."

"Gave her away!"

"Lend-Lease, a few years ago. She was loaned to the British in '40 to help them keep the se lanes open. Our cousins renamed her the *HMS Castleton*. We'll find out what happened to her after the war."

As we spoke, a metallic voice flowed through the PA system reminding us of another war.

**GUN CONTROL, BRIDGE. ROUTINE CHECK,
ON YOUR TOES UP THERE?
BRIDGE, CONTROL ALWAYS ON OUR TOES.**

The Chief handed me a second photograph. "There she is --- the *DD 483*. She was built in New Jersey and sailed for the Pacific in mid'42 --- for the Guadalcanal campaign. She sailed right up *Iron Bottom Sound*. That's where the Japs caught up to her."

"What happened?"

"She was bombed and strafed, and severely damaged. Damn near sunk. And on Friday, the 13th."

"Not a lucky day."

"She limped into a dry dock, made repairs and returned to duty. And got caught again. This time the Japs finished the job. Twelve planes jumped her in the *Slot*. Every gun fired until she sank."

THE SECOND U.S.S. AARON WARD

"Losses?"

"First attack, 15 killed, 55 wounded. Second attack, 27 killed, 59 wounded."

I didn't know what to say. Words, so useful to a journalist, seemed so ineffectual at this moment. I changed the subject ever so slightly.

"What about the third *Ward*?"
"Here."

Rossi handed me a third photograph. "Now we're closer to home. Yes, that's her. Launched 5 May '44 at the good old Bethlehem Steel Company.

THIRD U.S.S. AARON WARD

"Closer to the Pacific."

"She didn't have to cross the Equator if that's what you're referring to."

"Sort of…"

"The woman christening her the *DD 773*…"

"Yes?"

"I think she was the Admiral's great grand-daughter. That's another thing I've got to find out after the war."

A confused look covered my face, which the Chief saw.

"Trying to figure it out, Rob?"

"Well, yes. I thought we were on the *DM 34*."

"Well, you are and you aren't."

"Great, that cleared things up."

"Okay, the Navy decided it needed another "minelayer." The Navy converted the *DD 773* into the *DM 40* during construction. That's why we have tracks and lots of mines to sprinkle seas and hopefully drop an egg on a Jap sub. But it doesn't matter, The *DM 34* is all destroyer."

CIC, BRIDGE … HOW'S THE SCREEN?
BRIDGE, CIC… SCREEN IS CLEAR.
ALL CLEAR.

"History lesson is over, Rob."

I was reluctant to let go. I sensed something. Call it a reporter's hunch. A question kept bubbling up in my mind.

"Three *Wards* in 27 years! There's something you haven't told me, Chief."

"Pretty smart, aren't you?"

"Were you on all three *Wards*?"

"Why would you say that?"

"Reporter's intuition."

"You've found me out, son. Lied about my age to get into the First War. I was only 15 at the time, but big. Stayed in the Navy. Made it a career. Got wet with the second *Ward*. I'd like to keep try, if possible. And now here I am talking to you and still helping young "officers" to keep this hunk of metal afloat."

Hunk of metal, indeed… The Chief loved this ship as a man would a woman. The bond of affection was strong and enduring.

"I like dry and afloat," I said.
"Yeah."
"Chief, when the war is over, you should write a book about the *Wards*."

"Not me. You. But do me one favor."
"Yes?"
"Make me look dashing, handsome, and if there is any action, heroic."
"And do you want a beautiful damsel, too."
"Absolutely."
"My pleasure."

ADMIRAL AARON WARD

ROSSI'S STORY

He never married. The Navy was his life and his mistress. A couple times he came close to taking the dreaded vows. When the war ends, he's promised himself to consider matrimony if he can find that little lady who wants to shelter an old salt.

It was his job to turn the young recruits, most just out of high school, into warriors. Trained either at the Great Lakes Training Center or the one in Idaho, these kids were from everywhere and they were all looking for excitement on the high seas. It was the Chief's job to make sure they survived the excitement.

He took a special interest in Laverne Schroeder. Though he never quite said it, one had the feeling that he saw in the young man the son he never had. He pushed him hard believing that preparation and gun practice might keep the boy alive.

And he promised himself to retire once this mess was over.

Part V

BOGIES

THE ATTACKING PLANES

THE PILOTS

Chapter 21

LEAVES OF GRASS

FIRST DOG WATCH - 1800 HOUR

It was 6:00 p.m. straight up and I was quickly beating my way toward the bridge. Though the *Ward* was knifing cleanly through the calm seas at nearly 30 knots, there was a noticeable uneasiness aboard the ship. A sweaty quietness had taken hold of the crew. All hands seemed to be gathering their breath and strength, as if preparing for some great exhausting feat. The men, though occupied by their duties, sensed a lull, but before what? Everywhere sailors gave each other furtive looks. Laughter and joking were put away in lockers until the next day. Ribbing was exiled to the brig.

On the bridge, men took their cue from the Captain, who was sniffing the air, almost tasting it, trying mightily to fathom its airy depths. Something was out there. The men could see it in the Captain's eyes.

At the time, of course, I didn't know it, but deep within the ship in the crew's quarters, Laverne's copy of the *Leaves of Grass* by Walt Whitman was on his bunk opened to a special passage for all good sailor in all times. I often fantasized the words leaped into the heavens from the poet's ink pen and rained down slowly upon the *Ward*.

*FLAUNT OUT O SEA YOUR SEPARATE FLAGS OF
NATIONS!
FLAUNT OUT VISIBLE AS EVER THE VARIOUS
SHIP SIGNALS!*

The *USS Aaron Ward* as seen from above was on station, repetitiously
following an exact pattern, etched invisibly in RSP 10. The bow of the ship
cuts through the sea, separating the past from the present, always on duty.

*BUT DO RESERVE ESPECIALLY FOR YOURSELF
AND FOR THE SOUL OF MAN ONE FLAG ABOVE
ALL THE REST,*

The *Ward's* battle flags were raised, unfurled to the wind, a fabric of
tradition and duty, symbolic of the Navy's presence. Gleams of light etched
from the ship's anchors, tightly packed against the *Ward*, steel on steel, a
light shaft no longer symbolic of home and safety and peace. The uplifted
anchors announced a ship on duty in hostile waters.

*A SPIRITUAL WOVEN SIGNAL FOR ALL NATIONS,
EMBLEM OF MAN ELATE ABOVE DEATH,
TOKEN OF ALL BRAVE CAPTAINS AND ALL
INTREPID SAILORS AND MATES,*

In my mind's eye I saw Laverne his 20mm gun tub, unshielded,
unprotected. Behind a splinter shield, Norm Willis was exhorting his men
to prepare their 40mm weapon for action. Inside Mount 51, Al Warren's
crew was readying their 5-inch guns. Everywhere men and guns were
becoming one.

*AND ALL THAT WENT DOWN DOING THEIR
DUTY.
REMINISCENT OF THEM, TWINED FROM ALL*

*INTREPID CAPTAINS YOUNG AND OLD,
A PENNANT UNIVERSAL, SUBTLY WAVING ALL
TIME,*

O'ER ALL BRAVE SAILORS,
ALL SEAS, ALL SHIPS.

WALT WHITMAN

A MOTHER'S STORY

Danny's mother didn't want to be a Gold Star mother. Plain and simple, she didn't want the postman stopping at her door with a letter from the War Department. She didn't want a telegram from Washington informing her that her boy was wounded or missing or dead. She didn't want any communication beginning with, "We regret to inform you ..."

She didn't want to be a Gold Star mother. There were already enough of them in Elgin. She already had a white service flag with two blue stars stitched on it, one for Gabriel, her oldest son, and for Laverne, her youngest, to show that they're in the service. That was enough. She didn't want to add a

Gold Star to that flag. Devotion and pride and honor were fine, but she just wanted her boys home.

She had heard a lady on the radio speaking to Congress. She spoke for herself, but really, she spoke for all mothers.

"It was the mothers who suffered to bring these boys into the world, who cared for them in sickness and heath, and it was our flesh and blood that enriched the foreign soil. Can you picture the anxiety of these mothers --- the agony and suspense --- until they see their boys again? I don't think any man can feel the way a mother feels. It is a part of her body that is lying over there … She spends 20 years bringing up that boy; she gave him her time, both day and night. Who can realize what a mother's loss is like in war?"

She didn't want Laverne to go and she couldn't stop him. Gabriel had to go. All the boys were going. They had to go. I cried when Gabriel and Laverne left. I cry every night when I see their empty beds. I cry every morning when their breakfast plates are not on the table. I cry during the day when I'm doing my chores, when I think about them. Yes, I cry but I never show any tears.

Chapter 22

THE ATTACK

SECOND DOG WATCH -1822 HOUR

I was on the Bridge wearing a helmet and crowded into a corner out of everyone's way. I was comforted by the steel plates which formed my corner universe, protecting me like a mother's arms. I was trying to act calm, but the pounding in my chest and the sweat on my brow told a different story. I was experiencing fear again. It was a tangible monster that sought to devour me. Others on the Bridge were too busy to notice, or having noticed, too polite to say anything.

Looking back on it now, it all seems so unreal. Did all of what occurred really happen? Could my world have changed in such a short time, only 52 minutes? It must be true. It must have happened. Didn't the Navy say it happened?

THE OFFICIAL REPORT

THE OFFICAL NAVAL COMMUNIQUE FOR 3 MAY 1945 STATED THAT IN THE EARLY EVENING HOURS, FOUR SMALL GROUPS OF ENEMY AIRCRAFT ATTACKED OUR SHIPPING OFF

THE COAST OF OKINAWA INFLICTING SOME DAMAGE ON OUR FORCES. SEVENTEEN ENEMY AIRCRAFT WERE DESTROYED IN RSP 10 ... 26 DEGREES, 24 MINUTES N ... 126 DEGREES, 15 MINUTES E.

Inflicting some damage; how could the Navy say that? Small groups of enemy aircraft...! What was small about these groups? Yes, it was a communiqué, but brevity hardly explained what happened. You had to be there. You had to experience a lifetime in less than an hour. You had to be there for the "witching hour."

Much later, after carefully piecing together the events of that day, this is what happened, and what I would someday write about.

In the Radar Room, Kang was speaking to Lansing in a hush. "We've calculated bearing, estimated speed, distance of the bogies. They'll pass near us. Some one is sure going to catch hell tonight. I count at least thirty planes out there. Advise the Captain and all ships in the box."

"Captain, this is Lansing. Thirty or more planes headed our way."

"Understood."

One word ---understood --- conveyed a host of possibilities and stretched emotions. Would the planes turn away? If not, could the *Ward* fend them off? If unable to do that, would we be hit? If so, how bad would the damage be?

"What's our readiness, Bert? The Captain asked.

"We ready."

The officers and rated seamen listen as readiness messages come to the bridge, one reassuring message after another.

FORWARD ENGINE ROOM, MANNED AND READY ...

MIDSHIP REPAIR PARTY, MANNED AND
READY…

GUN DIRECTOR, MANNED AND READY.

ALL GUNS, MANNED AND READY…

On the bridge of the *LSMR 195…*

"Copy," Verso said. " Damn!"
"Maybe they'll fly south of us," a seaman said without conviction.
"Time to say your prayers, boys," Captain Atwood said under his breath.
"I wish we had unleaded those rockets two days ago," a voice muttered. Those things can't wait to go off."
"It will be one hell of a Fourth of July if they do," Verso explained. "We'll light up the damn whole neighborhood."
"Let's try to avoid that," Captain Atwood countered.

The *Ward's* radar detected the incoming raid at about 25-miles out. On the *Ward's* bridge, Captain Brown was receiving a constant stream of information.

CONTROL, CIC… TARGET BEARING 250,
SPEED 180…
CLOSING RAPIDLY. TRACKING.

Around the ship and high above the stacks, the lookouts finally spotted two Japanese planes, tiny dots on the horizon.

"Two planes, 20,000 yards out and coming in fast."
"The first plane bore down on the *Ward* --- 7,000, 6,000, 4,000 yards out. The *Ward's* guns opened up.

ALL GUNS, AIR ACTION STARBOARD, AIR ACTION STARBOARD.

The big 5 inch gun mounts opened up at 7,000 yards. Then smoke begins to trickle from one of the planes, but it kept on coming. At 4,000 yards, it dipped over into a dive and the 40 mm guns began firing. Tracers leap out of the guns, but the plane continued in its dive heading directly for the *Ward*.

RANGE THREE O DOUBLE O ... RANGE TWO 0 DOUBLE 0 ...

Two-thousand yards... The plane was almost upon them. Every 20mm gun was brought to bear on the target. Bullets burst from the guns in a last frantic effort to stop the plane, which was now skimming the water, coming fast. The noise was a constant blare of exploding shells rupturing the air. The kamikaze plane was hit again and again, and still it continued its suicide flight.

In Gun Mount 51, Warren yelled, "Fire! Fire point blank!"

Suddenly, the plane, a Zero, exploded right in their faces. A last desperate shot from the Gun Mount had done it.

"We got him," Warren screamed. "We got him. Splash one."

The plane exploded less than 100 yards from the *Ward*. As the flaming wreckage fells into the sea to end the kamikaze's death dive, the pilot was catapulted out of the cockpit and hurled high across the ship into the water on the opposite side. He looked like a mass of raw hamburger as he flew by. There was smoke everywhere caused by the dying plane. On the bridge, momentary relief now gave way to the unthinkable. Three pieces of the wrecked plane were still alive --- the engine, propeller, and right wing section were skidding across the last 50 yards of water. The propeller slammed into the after deckhouse. The wing sections crashed into the side of the ship near the rudder. The engine made a final skip, then flung itself into the air, and crashed into Mount 51, where it finally came to rest, twisted metal, still blazingly hot, harpooned into its killer.

The *Ward* was severely damaged.

JAP PROPELLER EMBEDDED IN WARD

"Out!" Warren yelled. "Get out! Now! We got to move whatever hit us. Our controls are all banged up." The gun crew swarmed out of the mount, trying frantically to get the engine away from the gun. Warren continued to yell at his men, even has Granados' damage control group ran toward them.

"Forget the blisters …Move the damn thing! Heave…!"

The engine was dragged out of the way. That's the good news. The bad news was …

CONTROL! MOUNT 51, HYDRAULIC-ELECTRIC SYSTEM OUT.. SHIFTING TO MANUAL CONTROL.

Manual control … Men would now have to move the 10,000 pound mount by hand gears. The mount was on its own…

From my vantage point, I surveyed the damage around me and quickly jotted in my note pad, *"… severe damage to Mount 51, one Kamikaze pilot*

151

has met his ancestors, and almost took out the Ward." Nearby, I saw the Captain, who had a quizzical look on his face.

"Where's the other plane?" he seemed to be asking.

The mess hall had been turned into a miniature hospital. Doc Ferrell and Little Bear were preparing for the first casualties. They could feel the ship twisting and turning under their feet. They could hear the guns above roaring and the fatal crash of the first Jap plane. They knew what that meant. Within a few minutes sailors would enter their world with the first of the wounded.

"Here we go, " Doc Ferrell said.

ALL GUNS, ACTION PORT, ACTION PORT!
RANGE EIGHT 0 DOUBLE 0
RANGE SEVEN O
RANGE SIX O

The gun tubs were a scene of organized chaos. Frantically, gunners were kicking empty cartridges out of the tubs. Others were checking the ready ammo racks preparing for the next attack already underway.

"Get ready," Willis cried, "get ready."

Laverne was almost too excited to speak, but his eyes conveyed his thoughts, "More ammo, my god, more ammo…"

In Mount 51, Warren was less hesitant to speak. He bellowed to his gun crew, who were turning the mount by hand, "Turn this damn thing."

On the bridge, I felt the fear reaching out to me, refusing to let me stand, forcing me to cower for a moment in my corner bunker. Yet, despite this, I willed myself to observe, to write, to remember.

The men on the bridge seemed so calm in the face of this attack, a stony feeling I coveted. For no apparent reason, I checked my watch. Only eight minutes had passed, but it seemed like an eternity.

COMMENCE FIRING!
COMMENCE FIRING!

The *Ward* responded with every gun bearing on the second attacking plane. To my horror, I watched as an intense cone of fire reached out to port, but impossibly, the second suicide plane seemed to ride the cone directly down toward the *Ward*. Though hit again and again, the Betty continued on. It refused to die. No one on the bridge could believe it.

"What's keeping that damn plane up?" Bert shouted.
"Maintain fire," the Captain commanded.

The plane itself, which had first been an insect in the sky, was now upon them, a metallic monster coming right at them. It seemed as big as a boxcar. There was no possible way to avoid it.

Two hundred yards off the *Ward's* bow, the *LSMR 195's* crew watched in desperation as the plane droned on in its death flight.

"Splash the bastard," Lopez screamed.
"Prepare to pull aboard survivors," Captain Atwood stated as if he were at a ball game calling in a reliever.
"All guns, fire if you have a target," said Verso.

I always wondered what the Japanese pilot saw and felt in those last few seconds as he fell upon the *Ward*.

The destroyer loomed up, becoming larger and larger. Shells were ripping into the plane, but somehow it didn't explode. A 20 mm shell cracks the cockpit

canopy. Blood was pouring from my shoulder. I could hardly see. The plane was twisting. I'm losing control of it. Only seconds now…Glory for the emperor.

The explosion was seen and felt by most of the *Ward's* crew. Somehow, against all odds, Mount 51 had done it again. Unlike the first plane, the flaming wreckage from this plane tumbled into the sea, only 1,200 yards from the *Ward*. All who witnessed the "miracle" uttered a silent prayer of "thanks," and vowed to take Warren's crew out to dinner next shore leave.

In my notebook, I wrote, "the biggest steak for those guys."

A reassuring message resonated throughout the ship causing me to think the worst was over.

CEASE FIRE!
CEASE FIRE!

I noted this order at 1831, "Cease Fire." Nine minutes had passed. We had survived the first onslaught. Only then did I think of the other destroyer, the *USS Little*. Much later I would learn her fate.

Apparently, low clouds shrouded the approach of at least five planes, providing the *Little* with less time to defend herself. Though the ship hit all the incoming planes, four kamikazes crashed into her in less than four minutes. The *U.S.S. Little* went dead in the water without power or communications. She was settling rapidly despite the crew's efforts to control the damage. The order was given to "abandon ship." In less than 12-minutes after the first plane attacked, the destroyer was gone. The human toll was great; 31 killed and 79 wounded, and many missing.

A third plane, undetected by radar and unseen by the lookouts, began its suicide run 6,000 yards out. It dove from the clouds astern of the *Ward*. The plane bore in, relentlessly. The entire ship was startled when the port twin 40mm guns just aft of the bridge opened fire without orders. Willis had spotted the threat. There had been no time for orders. On the bridge, Bert cursed for the entire crew, "God damn!" Every available gun with a bead on the plane fired away.

"We're not going to get him," the Captain said with only a slightly higher pitch to his voice.

"Look out," Chief Rossi yelled.

"Duck," screamed someone. Later, I realized I was the screamer.

What was keeping the plane in the air? It had been hit many times. Smoke was pouring from its left wing. Yet, the plane stayed intact. It seemed to increase in speed. Under its belly was a big, mean looking bomb, which was dropped about 100 yards away from the *Ward*. The bomb curved downward toward the port side of the ship. The plane, now aflame, followed the bomb, and crashed into the *Ward's* superstructure near the fantail, where it came to a screeching halt, half on and half off the ship.

Maintaining his log, Marcus wrote, "1831, ship hit by suicide plane.."

The *195* had closed in to the *Ward's* port side. The crew watched the crash and heard the resounding explosion. They saw fires break out and blackish smoke rising up from the *Ward*. Captain Atwood issued his orders. "Not good… Lets move in… It's time to go to work. Watch out for more bats."

The men on the bridge felt the impact as a dull thud. The ship trembled for a moment, and then sluggishly regained headway. It was apparent that the *Ward's* steering control was not responding. Something was seriously wrong. Each man had a different expression in response to the crash.

"Damage report, we need a damage report," Captain Brown demanded.

"What else is out there? Bert shouted to the heavens.

"Steering problems, 1832," Marcus whispered to himself as he made a log entry.

"We've got to toss that damn plane off the ship and now," Rossi yelled, half in English, the other portion in Italian.

The ship was beginning to lose steering control. The rudder was jammed hard left. She was chasing herself in a tight port circle like a mad dog. In doing so she was becoming a perfect target.

What had happened? How could one plane cause so much damage? The Jap bomb penetrated the hull below the waterline and detonated in the after engine room. Fuel tanks exploded resulting in a dangerous oil fire that cut steering control to the bridge. At the same time the rudder was jammed hard to port, forcing the ship to slow.

As to the LSMR-195... She was attacked by two suicide planes ... One struck home... It inflicted terrible damage, causing the stored rockets to explode. They went off, shooting off in all directions. The "little boy" was in danger of floundering.

For reasons I couldn't explain then or now, I stood up rather than remaining half perched behind my metal protection on the bridge, and screamed into the late afternoon sunlight, "How dare you do this to the *Ward*," even as I wrote those words in my note pad. The paralyzing fear seemed gone, as if this brush with death had erased it cleanly. The whole matter had simplified itself. If I was going to die, I would. One way or another, the heavenly vote was already cast. There was just no sense in worrying about it.

I glanced at Willis' 40mm tub and was shocked by what I saw. He had been blown out of his seat and thrown into a ready ammo rack, which kept him from flying overboard. He bounced back onto the deck minus both shoes, and one sock --- which in his bruised and dazed state he found slightly amusing. I'm sure those around him thought he had lost a few marbles as he scampered around looking for the missing sock..

"Where's my bloody other sock?" he kept yelling.

I almost laughed at Willis' antics, and then it hit me. Where was the bomb? I had seen the bomb fall! Where was it?

None of us could know it at the time. The 500-pound bomb had smashed through the *Ward's* main deck in front of the Bridge, then landed without an explosion in the crew's quarters. It had wedged itself there, and then inertness turned into an explosion below the water line. The *Ward* reeled and shook under the impact. The explosion tore a twenty-foot long hole along her port side.

The blast sounded like rolling thunder to the men in the Engine Room, which immediately began to flood. Ruptured oil lines were everywhere. They served to pour more fuel into the fires now raging out of control above and below deck. Stored ammunition, always a curse at when fire was present, threatened to explode in the intense heat. Telephone and power lines were broken. Circuit breakers and fuses went out. Darkness invaded the room and battle lanterns flickered on.

It was the *Ward's* deck, which now caught my attention. The deck was a sheer catastrophe. There were wrecked gun mounts with their weapons tipped at crazy angles, all but Mount 51. Torn steel plates, twisted cables --- fire and smoke, and exploding ammo seemed to be everywhere. Sprawled on the deck were the dead, and mixed in with them, the wounded.

One plane still clung to the *Ward*, a jumbled mass of scratched metal riveted to the ship it came to destroy. Beyond belief, the pilot of the suicide plane was still alive, slumped over and groaning in the cockpit. Granados' damage control party had reached the plane and extinguished small fires so that his crew could push the plane overboard. Helped by other sailors, the damage control party finally dislodged the inertia holding the plane to the deck. The danger of the plane blowing up was uppermost in everyone's mind. Finally, a mighty heave pushed the plane and the pilot over the side and into the accepting sea.

The damage control party was exhausted and relieved, but not yet done for the day. Desperate messages flashed back and forth throughout the ship.

AFTER ENGINE ROOM?
AYE. WE'RE FILLED WITH SMOKE BACK HERE.
THE ENGINE ROOM IS ON FIRE.
AYE. SECURE THE BOILERS. GET OUT OF THERE.

MOUNT 53, CONTROL. NO ANSWER.
MOUNT 52, CONTROL. NO ANSWER.
MOUNT 51, CONTROL. AYE, STILL FUNCTIONAL.
CONTROL STAY THAT WAY

On the Bridge the Captain stood stunned by the explosions and damage reports. Pleading to unseen gods, he cried out, "No more. Enough."

The gods were not listening.

Chapter 23

DELEGATE AND
MONGOOSE

SECOND DOG WATCH – 1835 HOUR

An American cruiser, code named *Delegate*, stood off shore at Okinawa. She was in command of all the *RPS's* circling the invasion fleet. *Delegate* was the nerve center, all antenna, radar, and in constant communication with all the ships on the stretched picket-lines --- mainly destroyers, minelayers, and "little boys.." Inside *Delegate's* CIC room, tight-lipped officers stared at a large plotting board. They were focusing on RPS 10, where black marks indicated the last known positions of the *Ward*, the *Little*, and the *195*.

"Situation is bad … *Ward* has been hit at least once," a grim-faced officer reported. "Many casualties. She is under constant attack."
"Sinking?" an older officer asked.
'Unsure?'
'The *Little and the 195?*"
"No word, yet."

Their conversation is interrupted by a message from the *Ward*, code named *Mongoose*.

> *DELEGATE, THIS IS MONGOOSE, OVER...*
> *WE ARE IN TERRIBLE SHAPE. WE HAVE BEEN*
> *HIT TWICE AND ARE STILL UNDER ATTACK.*
> *LITTLE HIT AND IN A BAD WAY. 195 HIT/ADVISE*

Immediately, a message was forwarded to the *Ward*.

> *MONGOOSE, HELP IS COMING. GOOD LUCK.*
> *DELEGATE, COPY THAT.*

"Too late to order a combat air patrol?" the younger officer asked.

"Almost sunset ... No time for a sortie. We'll contact what's in the area."

"They'll be flying in the dark soon."

"We've got to do something. Order the *Shannon* out there. She's been in the rescue business before."

"Two hours before she'll get to them."

"It's all we can do."

> *DELEGATE, THIS IS MONGOOSE. THE*
> *LITTLE HAS SUNK. THE 195 IS COMING*
> *UNDER SEVERE FIRE... TWO MORE PLANES*
> *SPLASHED.*
> *SEND ASSISTANCE NOW.*

Makalapa Crater in Hawaii was a tourist sight before the war. Now, three years into the war, it was Admiral Chester Nimitz's headquarters, the command center for the United States Navy in the Pacific Theater. The center was simply known as CINPAC.

At that precise moment, 3 May '45, 1840 hours, the Admiral was holding a high level meeting. Their topic was, as always, Okinawa, and the beating the Navy was taking from the suicide planes.

"These losses can't go on!" Nimitz said with emphasis.

"The DD's are taking a real clobbering," a bearded officer remarked.

"They're maintaining the RSP stations," a veteran staff officer offered. "But they're sitting ducks out there."

The Admiral asked, "How many of those damn suicide planes have attacked our ships to date?"

"Over 1500," the bearded one replied.

"Christ. How many more could they have? What does intelligence say?"

"Perhaps 2,000. Possible more."

"Hell, this could go on for months."

The meeting was interrupted by a young seaman … A decoded message was handed to the Admiral. He read the message before slamming the flimsy down on his desk. A forlorn look replaced the grizzled tough face the world had come to know.

THE LITTLE WAS SUNK

Command officers are used to the terrible costs of war. Every decision they make places ships in harm's way. No decision was immune from death. All they could do was carry on.

THE USS LITTLE

An officer went to a large map hanging on the wall. It showed Okinawa and the surrounding small islands, plus the RSP locations. He pointed to RSP 10.

"Air support will be minimal considering the time," he said. God help them."

"And their guns," the Admiral exclaimed. "And their guns."

KAMIKAZE ATTACK

Chapter 24

ACTION REPORTS

SECOND DOG WATCH - 1850 HOUR

I didn't remember getting hit. No bullet pierced my blue Navy work shirt or the orange life preserver over it. No jagged hole appeared in my helmet causing a fatal explosion in my head. It was just a tiny piece of shrapnel, which somehow flew through the air and impacted against my right leg. It felt like someone was pinching me for a moment. Only then did I sense a warm, wet feeling creeping down my trouser leg until a nerve decided to feel the pain.

Perhaps it was the randomness of it all that amazed and amused me even in this most terrible moment. An inch to the right or left and the hot metal bounces into a steel barrier or a wooden plank, or another sailor's flesh. An inch higher or lower and a small wound would be fatal.

I couldn't believe it. I was still alive. An unforgiving madness gripped me. And suddenly I was very angry. How dare someone try to kill me! I had my whole life ahead of me. I was going to be a great writer. This little war wasn't going to stop me. The Emperor's "bats" wouldn't stop me. I would be a writer.

Impressed with my own future and stunned by my own survival and resulting bellicose attitude, I hardly felt the medic working on me.

""Could have been worse. See Doc Ferrell later."

I looked around. The medic had gone on to help others on the bridge, including the Captain who was heavily bandaged around his right shoulder. Bert was bleeding from a wound in his left arm. The others --- Marcus and Rossi --- had also been hit by the explosion. The bridge, though still intact, was a mess.

The sun was nearly down now and gone, but not the battle. The sky and the sea were lethal backdrops to the affairs of men, and, as the planes and ships fought, no quarter was given. In the end, I realized, there would be only the living or the dead.

Long after the battle, Navy historians pieced together a series of "action reports," which provided an understanding of what happened next.

ACTION REPORT #1 – 1850

The *USS Little* had blown up. Three suicide planes crashed into her. In less than ten minutes she was gone. Thirty of her crew died with her. The *Ward* was the only destroyer left at RPS-10.

ACTION REPORT #2 – 1852

The *LSMR 195*, though damaged, was heading toward the *Ward*. It moved in closer, creeping towards the *Ward*, its hoses already pouring water onto the stricken destroyer, while others of its crew fished men out of the sea, some dead, many wounded or burned, all soaked, The air was thick with smoke.

PORT ENGINE OUT!
STEERING CONTROL LOST!

ACTION REPORT #3 – 1853

Granados' damage control party and repair gangs rigged fire hoses, running emergency phone leads where they could, fighting fires, and helping wounded men to the battle dressing stations.

ACTION REPORT #4 – 1855

Wounded men were everywhere in the mess hall --- on tables, lying on the floor, sitting in chairs. Injured men were flooding into the room assisted by medics. One seaman was carried in, stark naked with his skin hanging in shreds, his hair and eyebrows gone. It was a gruesome sight. It was apparent that there was far too many wounded sailors and not enough plasma, not enough morphine, not enough sulfa, not enough sterile needles. Not enough medics…

ACTION REPORT #5 – 1856

The Radar Room was relatively intact, undamaged. Men still peered intently at their screens, searching for blips; a common series of question pervades the room: "Where are they? How many more? What are they doing?"

ACTION REPORT #6 – 1857

Mount 51 had a problem. The twin breeches were chewing up the big 54 pound projectiles, firing almost non-stop. Without warning, one of them refused to slide into the firing chamber. The shell would not go in; the fuse in its nose had jammed. Warren looked at his crew; in a flash all understood. Down in the handling room, the fuse had been set for this projectile. No one in the Mount knew how many seconds were left before the thing would blow, destroying *Mount 51* and killing the entire crew. Frantic men now wrestled the shell loose and dragged it out of the gun. Wallace, big and tough, and redneck that he was, picked up the shell,

exited the Mount and heaved the shell overboard. With all the noise ---
guns firing, bombs exploding --- no one ever knew if the projectile blew.

ACTION REPORT #7 – 1858

A Zero buzzing above the ship suddenly dove on the *Ward* from about
8,000 feet. Again all guns still in action trained on the plane. The 5-inch
guns roared; the 40's barked; the 20's yapped. All fired in defiance. All
fired true. The *plane* started to smoke, but it continued to come in --- death
on the wing until finally, 2,000 yards out, it flipped over on its side, rolled
over the *195*, and then exploded before splashing into the sea. It has been
a near miss for both ships.

ACTION REPORT #8 – 1859

Magic and irony now combine in a tragic drama above *the Ward*.
Unexpectedly, three *Marine F4U's*, which had been sent out help *the Ward*,
broke through the clouds and came low over the water. Their running
lights were on to show they were friendly. But nervous gunners fired at
them anyway. The Marines hit their throttles to escape the *Ward's* guns.
They leaped into the sky and flew away at high speed. The *Ward* was left
alone, again without any air cover.

INCOMING

ACTION REPORT #10 – 1902

Shock and numbness have had their toll on the *Ward*. The near misses and direct hits have been too much. The fight has gone on for less than thirty minutes, yet it seems like hours --- like an eternity filled with guns clamoring, planes roaring, explosion and fire --- the stench of burning oil, the stench of burning men, the stench of a warship fighting for its life.

The forward fire room was flooding. This caused the *Ward* to lose all power and headway. The ship was a sitting duck and only her remaining gunners operating under manual control could function. Could they buy the ship enough time for repair crews to stem the flooding and put out the fires? Until then all the crew could do was to carry on.

ACTION REPORT #11 – 1903

Men were sweating to turn the ship around to face the new enemy. Every gear and mechanism needed to maneuver the ship manually was used by sailors in small, crowded rooms below deck. Muscle and grit were being used to compensate for the jammed rudder. Slowly, so very slowly, the *Ward* turned to face another onslaught.

ACTION REPORT #12 – 1904

A twin-engine Betty was 14,000 yards out flying barely above the waves. At 10,000 yards, Mount 51 opened fire, a long five miles from the plane. The *plane* had tried to sneak in unobserved, below the radar. Though spotted and fired upon, the plane bore in becoming larger and larger. Somehow it flew on through a curtain of fire, yet nothing seems to hit it. It was as if there is an invisible shield around the plane. Every still functioning gun was firing and reloading, firing and reloading. The *plane* flew on, 2000 yards, 1500 yards, 1,000 yards, and then 500 yards. Finally, Mount 51 scored a direct hit; the plane exploded, even as it crashed into the ship, a flaming mess, sliding along the damaged ship toward its tormentor, Mount 51.

ACTION REPORT #13 – 1905

Granados and his gang had seen and heard the explosion, which had cut down many sailors. There was fire and smoke everywhere. Wounded and dying men covered the blood-slick deck. Mount 51 was gone. Its two guns veered towards the deck. The Mount looked like a smashed house of cards. The *Ward* had too little to fight with now, only the 40mm and 30mm guns.

AIR ACTION PORT,
AIR ACTION PORT!

DAMAGED MOUNT 51

Chapter 25

MIRACLES

<u>SECOND DOG WATCH – 1913 HOUR</u>

A Val suddenly appeared out of the smoke, heading directly for the *Ward's* Bridge. The few guns left had trouble training on the plane. I watched as the planes loomed up in front of me, some 500 yards away. At a moment when he should be scared to death, I was strangely calm. I watched the plane as if I were at the movies, viewing an action packed Hollywood special. Sipping on a Coke Cola and munching on hot buttered popcorn, I felt himself watching a studio thriller emphasizing the genius of special effect technicians and actors. I felt like asking, "How do you do that?"

But this wasn't Hollywood. There was no soft drink, no popcorn, and no place to run and hide. I put my writing pad into my pants pocket. I was thinking, "I hope this survives even if I don't" Then, without realizing it, I yelled to the others.

"He's coming in! He's coming in! He's going to hit us."

At 300 yards, Chief Rossi contemplated his past and future, then resigned to his fate, yelled out, "You bastard, I was trying to make retirement." Having vented, he added practical advice to all who could hear.

"Get down. Cover your eyes!"

Bert crossed himself, hoping to make peace with his God. He accepted his fate as if he always knew it would end this way.

"Thy will be done ..."

For the Captain, though, there is no acceptance, no resignation. Anger clouded his face and his fists balled in some vain attempt to knock the bastard out of the sky. For reasons which I will never fully understood, he pulled, Old Admiral Ward's sword out of its case, and waved it at the incoming menace.

"Stay away from my ship!"

I could only watch. I couldn't stop what was about to occur. I watched Marcus still maintaining his report and knew what he must be writing: *"1908, bogie coming in ... Crash imminent."*

Every man on the bridge in particular, and many others throughout the ship, could see the plane. All felt the plane was coming directly at them. Oddly, one sailor, who was no longer firing a gun, threw his helmet at the plane as it flew down the ship's length. Another sailor fired a pistol at the pilot, who could be seen in the plane. Still another gestured in a universal fashion. Others simply cursed the demon plane.

I watched as the apparition loomed up in front of the Bridge, big as a house, its two exhaust pipes spitting blue fire. There was no way the plane could miss the *Ward*! Then, inexplicably the plane twisted in flight, banked slightly, and roared across the bridge, missing most of it.

The plane's left wing ripped out the signal flags, clipped the port forestay, and carried away most of the radio antennae. It smashed the top of the forward stack in a terrible crunch, and then cartwheeled into the sea to the starboard directly astern of the LSMR 195.

It missed the bridge. It was a miracle. It was at that moment that I gave up on agnosticism.

The certainty of death has been replaced by the capriciousness of events. The Captain was the first to respond to still another threat, yelling to Burt, "What are all those rocket explosions?

"The *195* ... been hit," Bert responded. "She's got a full load of rockets!"

"Maneuver away before ..."

As the rockets fired into the sky, exploding over both ships, I heard a familiar stanza ringing in my ears --- "By the rocket's red glare ..."

The *195*, though not directly hit, caught some of the plane's flaming wreckage, which ignited the ship's supply of rockets. Rockets went off in all directions, some hitting the *Ward* itself. As the smoke cleared, it was clear the *195* was in a serious way. She was taking on water. Amazingly, most the crew was still alive, though every man has some sort of wound. At that precise moment another suicide plane appears.

AIR ACTION...! AIR ACTION...!
DIRECTLY ABOVE!

Another Zeke was making an almost perpendicular strafing run. Its machine guns were spitting invisible bullets and very visible death. The shells bounced off the superstructure, and squirted through the air in every direction, lethal chunks of spent ammo still alive with death. It seemed like the Jap plane was going to go right down the stack.

And then came the miracle. At about 200 feet, the plane just blew up, exploding in every direction.

"What happened?" I asked dumbfounded.
"The rockets ..." Bert said still stunned by what he had just seen.
"The damn rockets got the it" Rossi shouted.
"Sixth plane destroyed by rockets from *195*," Marcus said as he wrote the same. To no one in particular, I said, "Thank you, Francis Scott Key."

Chapter 26

DAMAGE REPORTS

<u>SECOND DOG WATCH - 1918 HOUR</u>

The *195* was on fire. Her bridge was demolished. Wounded, but alive, Atwood has given the order to "abandon ship." Fire suppression was impossible. The rockets were a threat to everyone. With what steering and power he had, Atwood moved the *195* away from the *Ward*. As distance opened up between the ships, life rafts were thrown overboard. Men leaped into the oily water. At 250 yards, the officers left the ship. She had done her duty; they had done their duty. Two minutes later, *the LSMR 195* finally exploded, shattering the early evening with a final displace of fireworks and falling wreckage.

I saw all this from what was left of the *Ward's* bridge. Tears welled up in my eyes. I wanted to scream and shout, but no words came forth. Even as I watched, damage reports were flooding through the ship.

DAMAGE REPORT #1 – *LSMR 195*
LSMR 195. EXPLODED, 1918 HOUR. SINKING

DAMAGE REPORT #2 – RADAR ROOM
RADAR ANTENNAE WRECKED

SCREENS KNOCKED OUT
FIRE AND SMOKE IN ROOM

DAMAGE REPORT #3 – THE MESS HALL
FUNCTIONING
MANY WOUNDED, INCLUDING MEDICS
MANY DEAD, AT LEAST 20
SUPPLIES RUNNING LOW
LIGHTS OUT
USING BATTLE LANTERNS

DAMAGE REPORT #4 – THE ENGINE ROOM
BOILERS DROWNED OUT
ENGINES AT STOP
LITTLE STEAM LEFT
POWER LOSS, FLOODING

DAMAGE REPORT #5 – DAMAGE CONTROL TEAM
RUDDER GONE
STEERING GONE
HEADWAY GONE

DAMAGE REPORT #6 – ALL GUNS
ALL MOUNTS DESTROYED
HALF OF 40MM, 20MM TUBS GONE

The damage control reports painted a bleak picture. The *Ward* was essentially dead in the water, barely able to make a few knots. She could not be steered. She was a "sitting duck" for the next attack. And that attack came now against the almost defenseless ship. A *Zero* powered in astern against almost no opposition and slammed into the ship near *Gun Mount 43*, which was destroyed. Much later, the official Navy record of this moment would say:

The ship was dead in the water, the weather docks and superstructure aft of the bridge were a complete shambles, dead and dying men were tumbled in the wreckage, fire raged uncontrolled and in the inferno exploding ammunition made existence uncertain for those still left.

Those still alive already knew this. Their ship was a pile of floating junk. Everything seemed smashed; the stacks, guns, searchlight tower, gun turrets, the gun tubs --- smashed beyond recognition. Fire was raging on deck and below. The deck itself was now only a few feet above the water. And the sun was going down. May 3, 1945 was disappearing into history; the *U.S.S. Aaron Ward* was disappearing into history. The crew was disappearing into history.

But not without one final fight. Official Navy records captured the spirit of the effort.

Doc and his men bundled ... the badly wounded onto life rafts, and tied them alongside so they wouldn't get lost. They didn't have to reach down to the rafts; the ship was so low in the water they just reached across. The fire fighters, the repair gang, everyone able to help, fought fire, dumped
Hot ammunition, pushed weights overboard in an effort to help keep the ship afloat. They (the crew) were going to stay with her.

In utter contrast to the fighting, the sea was table calm, a black mirror on which floated the debris of ships and empires, and the corpses of sailors and suicide pilots. The sea somehow seemed to accept all.

STILL AFLOAT, STILL FIGHTING

Chapter 27

THE SWORD

The *Ward* was dead in the water, listing five degrees to port. She had been under constant attack now for almost one hour. Six suicide planes had crashed against her bulkhead. At least that number had been shot out of the sky. What more could be asked of the ship and its crew? On what was left of the bridge, the Captain pondered another question: *"Should he abandon ship?"* As he considered the question, he noticed something shiny still grasped by his hand. He gazed at the sword for a long moment, thinking aloud, "What would the old Admiral do?" He held the sword in his hands, then looked around the battered bridge and its injured crew still on duty. He raised the sword into the twilight sky, an answer on his determined face.

"Hell, no!"

Somewhere in the recesses of history, I think, Old Aaron Ward stirred, as did John Paul Jones. *The U.S.S. Aaron Ward* would fight on. And fight on she would. At that moment, the radio cracked on, the reconnected lines breaking up in static.

AIR ACTION STARBOARD,
AIR ACTION STARBOARD!

179

A last suicide plane, hidden in a pall of smoke, appeared out of the increasing darkness. It was coming in low over the water from the stern, from the fantail. What few guns could still operate fire blindly through the night in one last supreme effort to knock down this last kamikaze, which was now 5,000 yards out and coming fast. Everywhere on the burning and blistered ship, men turned to see the new threat, now approaching them.

FIRE AFT.
FIRE AFT.

The Zeke was 3,000 yards out. A lucky hit… Smoke poured from it. She was slowing. Somehow the *Ward's* gunners had hit it. But somehow the pilot was keeping his plane in the air. Everything seems to be happening in slow motion.

ALL GUNS, FIRE!
ALL GUNS, FIRE!

"We can't fight from here."

The Captain, sword in hand, hobbled off the bridge, and limped his way toward the fantail. I followed. I can't tell you why.

Wounded and defiant, the Captain slashed at the night air with the sword, loudly yelling, "You will not have my ship." Tired and exhausted sailors watched their Captain. Tears welled up in their eyes, but not from the smoke. They took heart from him, and quietly, as one, vowed to fight on, to never surrender the ship.

The last intruder was now at 1500 yards and firing its machine guns, strafing the *Ward's* deck. The Captain was at the stern of the ship, standing on the junk that was once the fantail. Wounded men were all around him, placed there by Doc Ferrell for transfer to the now destroyed *195*. The ship's flag, *Old Glory*, now barely attached to its standard, was tattered and singed, but still fluttering in the breeze.

ALL GUNS …
ALL GUNS …

180

The Zeke's bullets reached out and hit the Captain. To avoid falling to the deck, he clutched at the flag. Unable to bear his weight, the flag tore loose from its ropes. As the Captain and the flag began falling to the deck, I arrived and grasped both, and gently lowered them to the still hot steel plates. A gust of wind whipped the flag around him, draping him in its folds.

"Captain ..."
"Help me up."
"You're wounded."
"Now. That's an order."

I lifted the Captain to a standing position. It was obvious he was seriously wounded.. Around us, those who have seen this drama silently cheered their Captain as he again raised his sword in defiance. Those still able continued to fire away.

Clinging to me, and cloaked in the flag, the Captain spoke his last words before collapsing.

"Tell our story."

The *Zeke* was now 500 yards out. The geometry of war was beyond doubt --- the planes glide path, the *Ward's* headway ... Converging lines ... The fate of ship and plane were now one; both must surely die.

Behind me was Laverne. He had climbed out of his damaged tub. He was holding a 20mm gun and focusing it on the Zeke. Standing in the midst of wounded sailors on the fantail and in sight of the dead Captain, Laverne took aim on the incoming plane and fired. The plane was less than 150 yards from the ship. He continued to fire in short bursts until he was out of ammo. He flung his weapon into the air at the invader. The Zeke, though hit by Laverne's fire, was almost on top of them, less than a football field away and blasting away with its machine guns. Strafing bullets found Laverne and knocked him to the deck, where he remained with a bloody spot on his chest.

The end had come. The damaged plane was going to crash on the *Ward*. The Captain and Laverne, fallen comrades in arms, rested forever on the *Ward's* deck. Still almost untouched by bullets and bombs, I gripped the flag and watched the suicide plane plunge toward me.. There is nothing else I could do. I was going to die with the Captain and the youngster. I remembered thinking, "I'm in good company."

In the last second, the Zeke's right wing began to fall away and it flipped over on its side and veered off to the leeward, barely missing the *Ward*. It fell into the sea, the last attacking kamikaze at RSP 10. Somehow Danny's 20mm gun had saved the ship.

The battle was over. The *Ward* would live if the battered crew could keep her afloat and no more suicide planes arrived.

I looked over at Laverne. Kneeling next to him was Granados. His hands were out in front of him, held high in the act of prayer.

"Lord, I beseech you… Honor thy kingdom with this soul."

SURVIVORS IN FRONT OF THE JAPANESE PROPELLER

Chapter 28

OFFICIAL REPORTS – AUGUST 3, 1945

I was sitting in a tidy, but small room at Naval Base in Honolulu. On the large desk before were many papers --- official documents, personal notes, and newspaper accounts concerning *the U.S.S. Aaron Ward*. I had been given permission to research the material in order to write a history of the ship. Admiral Nimitz himself had made this possible.

"Why me? I had asked the Admiral.

"Three reasons, Mister. First, you were placed on the *Ward* to tell its story. So tell it."

"And?"

"You were present during the attacks. You owe it to your fallen shipmates."

"And the Captain?"

"Yes."

"The last reason?"

"You survived."

One doesn't say no to a Fleet Admiral. I didn't.

Others had classified and categorized the materials, mainly battle reports in an orderly fashion in preparation for my research and writing. It was three months to the day and I was about to relive the battle.

REPORT #1 – THE SEA – SECOND DOG WATCH – 2000 HOUR

The battle was over ... The sea around us looked as it had a hundred years before, as it would a thousand years from now. This was different than a land battle where grass can eventually cover the scars of war. Here the sea cleaned up things in a few minutes. The reminders of ships and sailors war was either floating away or disappearing beneath the ocean's dark surface. In time, there would be almost nothing to show what had taken place at Radar Picket Station 10 --- the savage violence, the ships and planes lost, the many sailors wounded and dead.

In time all traces of the battle would be cleansed by sea. It was quiet now, out there where planes and ships had fought. A full moon probably glanced down in silence as it moved on through shifting puffy clouds, which hung silently above the waters.

REPORT #2 – LIGHTENING THE SHIP –NIGHT WATCH - 2100 HOUR

Chief Marcus wrote the report before me. Though wounded twice, he had prodded his fellow sailors in the aftermath of the battle.

I pushed the men hard in the immediate hours after the battle ended. I had to. We were listing. The ship was in danger of sinking. Our first job was to jettison topside weight whatever it might be --- ammunition, loose wreckage, anything that could be dumped overboard to lighten the ship, I was fearful that, if the ship floundered, our men would be in real trouble in the water. Almost all of our life rafts and floater nets had been torn or burned. Only one whaleboat was available, still hanging in the davits at a rakish angle. You've got to remember that lots of guys in the Navy don't know how to swim and all of us were afraid of the sharks. So I pushed the men hard.

REPORT #3 – NIGHT WATCH - 2200 HOUR

Coke-Cola … Would you believe it? At the risk of sounding like an ad for the Coke Cola Company, Elmer's scribbled report explained how he saved the day.

In his own way Elmer added a chapter to the *Ancient Mariner*. He knew that thirst at sea was a terrible thing. In the heat of battle and in the struggle to keep the *Ward* afloat, few men had anything to drink. Now when they could drink, there was no water. Pipes were fractured, tanks were ripped open or contaminated, and the pumps weren't working.

Before we left Frisco, I stored cases of Coke-Cola in the bowels of the Ward for happier moments. It turns out I stored them real well. I got a few guys together and we began to bring up the sealed bottles, first a few at a time, then by the case. For the men, it became a precious drink to slake their thirst. The guys who went below for it were brave men. The ship could have gone under anytime. Beneath the deck, they wouldn't have had a chance. I think the crew became lifetime Coke Cola drinkers that night.

REPORT #4 – DAMAGE CONTROL TEAMS – NIGHT WATCH - 2250 HOUR

Granados' report was straightforward. He and his men had never been trained for what they were dealing with. But deal with it they did.

My men worked with their bare hands, axes, crowbars, strong metal cutters and flashlights in near dark conditions. Most of their clothes were ripped and burned; all of them seemed to have cuts and bruises; they were all tired and hungry and thirsty. Below deck we fought the flooding and fires in a world where hoses twisted about like dead snakes, where one feared touching something too hot, or stepping into a hole and falling into an abyss. No one wanted to meet a dead sailor, a buddy … Until we got the pumps going and slowed the flooding, we feared for our lives.

REPORT #5 – THE *U.S.S. SHANNON* – NIGHT WATCH - 2300

The *U.S.S. Shannon, DM 25*, was first on the scene. She had been dispatched to assist the *Ward*. What follows was the vivid description of what she saw as she approach the stricken ship.

Was that a ship? The hull was unlighted. The main deck was almost at water level. Fitful glows of battle lanterns appeared through ragged holes where sailors were clearing away wreckage. It was difficult to make a ship out of the crazy mess of torn metal. The port side aft was just a heap of rubble. The forward stack had been smashed almost flat. Pieces of Japanese aircraft cluttered the deck. Pieces of deck guns still pointed at the sky. The night was rank with the stench of battle --- spilled fuel oil, blistered paint, overheated guns, burnt mattresses, sweat, blood, and seared flesh.

REPORT #6 - THE TEKESTA – MID WATCH - 0440 HOUR

The *Shannon's* job was to tow a 2,200 ton ship forty-five miles into Kerama Retto, a small island near Okinawa, which the Navy used for repairing ships. Because she was dragging the *Ward* like a harpooned whale, the *Shannon* could make no more than five knots per hour. The two ships crawled through the night, always fearful that a rogue suicide plane might come upon them, or an undetected submarine would spot them. Linked together by a long chain, the two ships would have no chance. It would prove to be a long, slow ride.

Eventually, the two ships reached *Kerama Retto*. A little tug, the *Tekesta*, came out to meet them. She made fast to the *Ward's* starboard bow, and then fed the half-starved sailors. The *Tekesta's* crew passed over big pots of hot coffee, loaves of bread, chunks of cheese. It was a great breakfast --- for the living. The *Tekesta* then took over for the *Shannon* and pushed the *Ward* through the crowded anchorage to a spot assigned to her. The Captain of the *Tekesta* filed this report about how the *Ward* looked.

Our crew, as did the crews of other ships in the harbor, looked down on the dirty, ragged, bloody crew; on the indescribable wreckage; on covered forms on the forecastle; on burned bodies still trapped in the debris. We saw a terrible sight.

One warship anchored nearby, the *U.S.S. McKinley*, which was the flagship for the fleet, signaled the *Ward* by searchlight. The message read:

Congratulations on your magnificent performance.

The message came from *CINPAC*. It came from Admiral Nimitz himself.

REPORT #7 – HOME – WEEKS LATER

The *Ward* had sustained a "stateside hit," meaning her damage could only be repaired in a mainland Naval yard. After necessary repair work for the trip to California, the ship left for San Diego on one engine. Calm seas and no suicide planes eased the trip back to a familiar coastline, first Pearl Harbor, then the Coronado Islands, and later Point Loma, before reaching San Diego. As the *Ward* neared Ballast Point, two new big, fast destroyers passed as they headed to sea. They were trim and ship shape, guns bristling, and businesslike. Many on the *Ward* wondered aloud how the ships would react to seeing a banged up minelayers drifting past them. The official record indicated the following:

To the surprise of most Aaron Ward's men and the everlasting pride of all, the lead destroyer piped "ATTENTION TO PORT," her companion followed suit, and both ships rendered honors as they passed. The Ward might have been a battleship, or a cruiser carrying the President.

The *Ward* was home. Though most of the crew had forgotten it, each man had taken an oath when he enlisted and when the ship had been commissioned. As they headed into port, survivors of a terrible fight, every man could say in good conscience, *"I met the test of this oath."*

I ... DO HEREBY SWEAR ... TO BEAR TRUE FAITH AND ALLEGIANCE TO THE UNITED STATES ... AND TO DEFEND HER AGAINST ALL ENEMIES ..."

Part VI

TWILIGHT

A NAVY IS NOT A PROVOCATION TO WAR. IT IS
THE SURST GUARANTY OF PEACE.
                    PRESIDET THODORE ROOSEVLT

Chapter 29

FINAL RESPECTS

We stood together, Lansing and myself next to the anchor and chain. The sword and the flag rested against the relics, one of steel, the other of fabric. We were two old men who had done their duty. We had kept our promise. Standing there, we were bathed in the last waning rays of the late afternoon sun, which continued to remind us of another sunset 50 years ago.

"So long ago," Murray said. "So long ago."

"Yes."

"Looking back, it hardly seems possible …"

"… that it happened."

"… that anyone survived …"

"Forty-two guys never made it," I reminded him.

"And over 100 wounded."

"But we made it home," Murray said. "Remember, they called us heroes when we reached San Diego?"

"We were very young. All the compliments sounded so good.

"It took us awhile to figure out who the real heroes were."

"The guys who didn't come home."

"Yeah."

"And then came the junkman from New Jersey," I commented. "What did he pay for the *Ward*?"

"$38,000 for a destroyer that cost $6-million to build."

"Solid deal for the junkman."

As we spoke a school bus slowly wound its way toward the brow of the cemetery, toward the military portion of the cemetery. Printed on the side of the bus was *Elgin School District*.

"I sure miss the guys," I said to Murray.

"The reunions helped."

"Yes. Beer, wives, and stories."

"Your book was great."

"My great American war novel?"

"For our crew, yes."

I shrugged. What could I say? As Murray pointed out, *Miracle at RPS 10* had been a big hit with the crew, and a few volumes had been sold to colleges and libraries, but it never made it to the *Book-of-the-Month* list. The critics had liked it, but not the general public, and certainly not Hollywood. Still, a documentary had been made on the basis of the book and some school districts had even bought it. Who knows, maybe it will end up on a new fangled cable station. Wouldn't that be something?

"When we're gone…" I said.

"What," a distracted Murray replied.

"Will anyone remember what happened? I asked. What we did? What's in the book?"

"Our kids?"

"Others?"

"Who knows?"

The school bus had stopped about twenty-five yards from them. High school students were quietly exiting the bus, along with their teacher, a middle age woman. The students were gathering around their teacher.

"I think we're about to be invaded," Murray announced.

"A field trip of some sort."

"We better finish up."

"Right."

I pulled from my pocket a worn piece of paper, which was entitled *Presidential Unit Citation to the U.S.S. Aaron Ward.* I held the paper so that we could both read it.

"We'll read it together as planned," I told Murray.

"Let's do it."

For extraordinary heroism in action as a Picket Ship on Radar Picket Station during coordinated attacks by approximately twenty-five Japanese aircraft near Okinawa on May 3, 1945 …

About twenty high school students and their teacher stood by their bus watching us. We could not avoid their presence. It was hard to concentrate. In their minds, I thought, they must be wondering what are those two old men doing reading something by the anchor and chain. The writer in me fantasized a female student saying, "It looks like those guys beat us here today."

"Yes, it does seem that way," the teacher said.

Had I been privy to the teacher's thoughts, I would have heard her say, "Those men… They seemed vaguely familiar to me. Who were they? What were they doing here today of all days?

Shooting down two Kamikazes which approached in determined suicide dives, the U.S.S. Aaron Ward was struck by a bomb from a third suicide plane as she fought to destroy this attacker before it crashed into her superstructure and sprayed the entire area with flaming gasoline.

The teacher and her class walked toward the two men. A young man spoke to his teacher.

"Look at that sword. It's just like the one you told us about."

Another student added, "And there's the flag you read to us about from the book."

A third student could hardly contain himself. "There's the anchor and chain just like it was in the film we saw."

An old childhood memory was forming in her mind. She had seen these men before. To her students, she quietly said, "When we get there, remember to be very respectful."

Instantly flooded in her after engine room and fire room, she battled against flames and exploding ammunition on deck and, maneuvering in a tight circle because of damage to her steering gear, countered another coordinated suicide attack and destroyed three kamikazes in rapid succession.

The students and their teacher stopped at the monument. Quietly and respectfully as requested by their teacher, they form a semi-circle around the men, who seemed at this moment to be oblivious to their presence --- as if they were somewhere else. For the first time, the students could see that the men were reading something. They could also hear the words read.

Still smoking heavily and maneuvering radically, she lost all power when her forward fire room flooded under a seventh suicide plane which dropped a bomb close aboard and dived in flames into the main deck.

Almost at once, it dawned on the students that these men were talking about what they have been learning in class, about the war and a ship. Under his breath, one student asked his teacher, "Are these men from the ship you've been telling us about?"

Unable to recover from this blow before an eighth bomber crashed into her superstructure bulkhead only a few seconds later, she attempted to shoot down a ninth Kamikaze diving toward her at high speed...

The students listened intently. Who are these men? One female student turned to the teacher to ask, but the words stuck in her throat. Tears were streaming down her teacher's face.

... and, despite the destruction of nearly all her gun mounts aft when this plane struck her, took under fire the tenth bomb-laden plane, which penetrated the dense smoke to crash on beard with a devastating explosion.

The students are entranced. They know about this. They have been learning about this ship for the past week in preparation for ...

With firers raging uncontrolled, ammunition exploding and all engine spaces except the forward engine room flooded as she settled in the water and listed to port ...

The teacher, through tearful eyes, was looking at the cover of a book, which she gripped tightly. A look of recognition slowly clarified for her. She knew who these men were and what they're doing here today.

... she began a nightlong battle to remain afloat and, with the assistance of a towing vessel, finally reached port the following morning.

The semi-circle had imperceptible tightened around us. We could feel the presence of the students.

By her superb fighting spirit and the courage and determination of her entire company, the Aaron Ward upheld the finest traditions of the United States Naval Service.

James Forrestal,
Secretary of the Navy, 1946

I carefully folded the paper and replaced it in my pocket. On cue, we snapped to attention and saluted the monument. We held the salute for one full minute in the stillness of the twilight hour.

Around them, the students stared in absolute awe.

"We're done," I said.

For the first time, we actually saw the students and the teacher.

"Mr. Rosenthal...? she said tentatively.
"Yes. Do I know you?"
"You don't remember me."
"I ..."
"Why would you? I was a little girl she remarked with a little nervous laugh. I met you at a reunion, back in 1960, I think, in San Diego. I was 10 years old.
"San Diego," Murray repeated.
"My grandfather brought me to it."

The students were watching, spellbound. This was history, not the history of the textbook. This was the real thing.

"Your grandfather ..." I said.
"Yes, to learn about an uncle I never met."

Murray and I looked at each other. Something unplanned was happening for which they were totally unprepared.

"Who was your uncle?" I asked.

The teacher looked at us, then focused on me. She held up the book she was carrying.

"You wrote about him in your book."

For the first time I noticed the book in her hands --- my book, a history of the *Aaron Ward* --- "*Miracle at RPS 10.*" On the backside, was my picture, a younger me over forty years ago.

"Your uncle's name?" I asked again.

"I never really knew him ... I only heard about his from my father and grandfather."

"Please, Your uncle's name ..."

"Laverne Schroeder."

"You were Lavernes's niece?" I commented more than asked. What is your name?"

"Gabriella Jackson. I was named after my father, Gabriel, who was Danny's older brother."

"And these students... Why are they here?"

The teacher held up my book and said, "For the same reason you are; it's the 50th anniversary of the attack on the *Ward*. I wanted my history students to know about Laverne and his ship and what happened. I used your book to help me."

"This is unbelievable," I said a bit too loudly. "Unbelievable."

"I had another reason."

"Which was?"

"I made a promise to do this before my father passed away three years ago."

"We didn't know about the promise," Murray said.

The students were crowding around their teacher and the two men. One of them, a little shy, asked in a small voice, *"Would you tell us about the flag?"* Another student added, *"And the sword?"* Still one more student joined in with a question, *"And the anchor and chain?"*

Murray and I glanced at each other and then at the students.

"Oh, yes," I said. "Do we have a story to tell? It all began in 1946, July of that year, when a warship was decommissioned and sold for scrap, and a fellow by the name of Schroeder decided to buy the ship's anchor."

APPENDIX

RADAR PICKET STATIONS (RPS)

The first line of defense against the kamikaze attacks. RPS-10 is easily identified on the western edge of Okinawa, isolated and vulnerable to suicide planes.

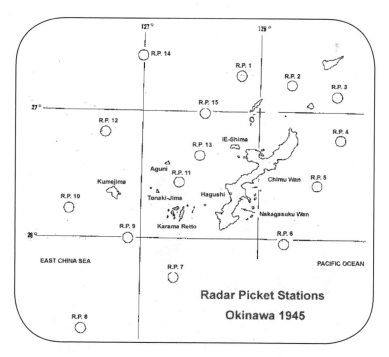

KAMIKAZE ATTACKS – MAY 3, 1945

The diagram below indicates the Japanese "hits" on the USS Aaron Ward during the 52-minute battle.

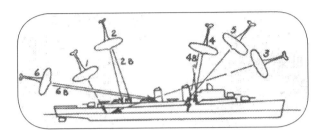

HITS

1. Near miss crash. Engine and propeller hit Mount 3.
2. A Zeke hits Mount 4. A bomb hits the outside of the engine room.
3. A near crash damages the N. 1 stack.
4. A VAL hits the main deck.
   4B. Near miss in side of forward fire room.
5. A VAL crashes into the deckhouse.
6. A kamikaze hits the after stack.
   6b. Another plane crashes in same area.

JAP ENGINE ON THE WARD'S DECK

PROPELLER BURIED IN THE WARD

THE L.A. TIMES REPORTS

THE HAMS CASTLETON

The first *Aaron Ward (DD – 132)* fought in World War I. Between wars the ship was mainly in the reserve fleet. On September 30, 1939, the ship came out of the reserve. She reentered the active Navy to assist President Roosevelt's to protect the Western Hemisphere as part of a Neutrality Patrol after the outbreak of war in Europe. She conducted neutrality patrols in the Gulf of Mexico and in the West Indies. On September 9, 1940, the *Ward* was decommissioned at Halifax, Nova Scotia. She was transferred to Britain as part of the President's policy to loan 50 older destroyers to London to fight the German submarine menace. She was commissioned the same day as *HMS Castleton*. Following the war she was sold for scrap, March 6, 1947.

THE FIRST AARON WAR

Printed in the United States
by Baker & Taylor Publisher Services